MW01131393

Also by Gary Cook…

The Old Man

Oak Seeds: Stories from the Land

Wounded Moon

CHANCE OF RAIN

CHANCE OF RAIN

Gary Cook

For Jackie —
Thanks!

Gary Cook
7/28/21

For Karen, who swims the lake every day,
and always comes back to me.

CHANCE OF RAIN

CHAPTER 1

No matter how we try to hide it, we live in a savage society. Still. For thousands of years we have tried to climb above it, push it behind us, declare it historic. Murder. Blood. Rape. Rage. Robbery. Fear. Kidnapping. Terror. The purposeful departure from goodness is all around us and we must deal with it. Deal with it. Take the darkness in and roll it around in our hearts and deal with it. Society boasts a solution to crime with badges, arrests, trials, convictions, and prison, but those ideas of containing violent behavior do nothing for the unrest in my heart. The justice system builds a make-believe box in which I can throw my unrest and try to forget the pain of dealing with it, but it is like trying to keep a ping-pong ball submerged in a swimming pool...easy at first, but impossible over time. Now that time has passed since Samuel's murder, I feel the strain of keeping it pushed down.

Ultimately, my spirit has to deal with the fact that I want to kill them. The murderers of my young friend need to die. Their dark lives are repulsive to good people, no different than cancer or crack cocaine or rancid food in the refrigerator. They should die; no, I want to kill them and that very thought makes me dark...a part of them. I fight that darkness and push the ping-pong ball back down. Vengeance is mine, sayeth the Lord, and then Jesus whispers in my ear, "Forgive them...give me your pain."

I blinked and Ella was standing at my office door watching me. She wore a black cotton dress and flats.

"You haven't moved a muscle in twenty minutes," she said.

"You're over-protective," I answered. "And you streaked your hair."

"Don't change the subject," she said.

"Okay," I said. "I love your hair."

She moved to the chair in front of my desk and sat knees together and arms crossed. "You're going to do it, aren't you?"

"Yep."

"I'll quit if you leave here," she said. "I swear, Ethan Stewart. I'll quit."

"No, you won't," I said taking a sip of cold coffee. "You've run this office for the last three chiefs and this division would fall apart without you."

"True," she said. "And that's why when I quit, it'll be on you, the demise of this outfit, and besides, the two chiefs before you were figureheads. You, on the other hand, are the real deal."

I smiled. "You've never used flattery before. It lessens your intimidating presence."

"I can use the truth anyway I choose. I don't offer flattery very much because you'll think I have a thing for you."

"You don't?" I said.

"No."

"Then we can't have an affair?" I said.

She stood, walked to the door and looked back.

"Everyone who knows you well, knows you are still married, Ethan. The ring is still on your finger and it's been what, a year now?"

I looked at the ring, the gold edges worn and rounded from thirty years of wear. "It won't seem to come off," I said.

"I'll quit," she said again and returned to her desk outside my office.

The phone rang two minutes later and her voice was professional as usual, with no hint of our previous conversation. "A Mr. Nichols from Houston County," she said.

"Regarding?" I ask.

"A house," she said flatly.

"Oh," I said.

"I'll quit. I swear it," she said for the fourth time before transferring the call.

"This is Ethan Stewart."

"Mr. Stewart. This is Phillip Nichols from over here in Houston County and Sam Lingo said you were interested in buying a house on White Oak Creek."

"I am," I said. "Wondered who owned it."

"Her name is Taylor James. She won't sell, I'll guarantee it. Strong-willed woman. I've tried to buy it for years. She won't sell, but I have a real nice house in the same area you should take a look at..."

I wrote the name down as I spoke, wondering if her parents were fans of James Taylor. "This other house...it on a hill?"

"Kinda," he said.

"Oaks in the yard?"

"Some, yeah," he said.

"Got a creek running next to it?"

"Ah, no, but White Oak Creek is about a mile away."

"Sorry," I said. "Gotta be on the creek."

"Those are hard to find," he said. "You should really take a look at this other house...."

"I suppose that's what makes them valuable," I said.

"What?"

"That they're hard to find," I said.

"She won't sell that house, Mr. Stewart."

"You said that before," I said.

"And it's the truth."

"Thanks for your time," I said.

I walked outside my office and handed a note to Ella. "I have a meeting with the Director now. Would you please find a number for this lady in Houston County?"

She looked at the note. "How hard is it to call information?" she said. "Oh, I forgot, secretary work…is beneath you."

I leaned over and kissed her on the cheek. "Ten dollars says she's unlisted," I whispered in her ear.

"Another ten says she plays guitar," she said looking at the name.

"You're on. And I bet the lady can't sing a lick," I said.

"Is that all you want? A number and address?"

"No, I want everything you can find about her using your advanced law enforcement skills."

"You turning me loose on this?" she asked.

"Yep…within legal guidelines, of course."

"When you get back, I'll know her cup size," she smiled.

I rode the elevator down to the first floor, crossed the lobby, decorated with expertly mounted deer, bear and turkeys and entered the Director's office. His secretary smiled at me professionally.

"Morning, Ethan. You're lucky; he just got off the phone."

"Was it a good call or bad call?" I asked, trying to judge his mood.

"Wasn't a politician or commissioner. You should be okay," she said.

I knocked on the open door jam. He looked up. "Come in, Ethan. How's everything?"

"Mornin,' James," I said. "Got a few minutes? It won't take long. "

"You never do take long. That's the thing about you, Ethan. Never remember a conversation with you that lasted more than ten minutes."

"Ten minutes will handle most subjects, don't you think?" I said.

James smiled. "Some of my staff could spend an hour on the merits of a one-minute egg."

I paused and placed a folded letter on his desk. "That's a request for transfer to the open officer position in Houston County," I said without smiling.

"Who's requesting the transfer?" he asked.

"I am."

The Director did not touch the letter, but removed his glasses and rubbed his eyes. His smile fell and then got real big and I noticed his hair was thinner than years ago and his wrinkles were deeper. "That's real funny."

"I'm serious," I said. "I think the HR guys call it a retreat."

"I know what it's called," he said softly. "Sit down." He paused and then just looked at me with a finger against his lip. "Hmmm," he uttered finally.

"I'm serious," I said again.

He reached up and loosened his tie. "Bad idea, Stewart," he said.

Neither of us said anything for a few seconds. He just looked at me.

"Look," he said. "You've had a rough year. It's understandable that you would be confused, but you've been chief of law enforcement for ten years. You are highly respected. You know more about constitutional law than any two attorneys I know. The men like you or at least respect you." He shook his head. "And you want to go back to where you started twenty-five years ago. Entrance level game warden."

"Yep," I said. "I do."

"Why?" he asked.

"Seems right to me," I said.

He paused again looking at me. "Have anything to do with the death of our officer in Houston County?" he asked.

"Murder. Samuel was murdered," I said. "But this request is not about that."

"The hell it's not," he said.

"No sir. I would just like to finish my career where I started. No politics or administration. Just catching bad guys."

"Well, I won't approve it," he said quickly.

"I don't think you can stop me, with all due respect," I said.

"I can do anything I want for the good of the agency," he said. "I'm the Director."

"Yes sir, you can. But if you don't approve the transfer, I'll quit. Or you can fire me. But I don't believe you will."

"Why, Ethan? No bullshit. Why?"

"I like the idea of it," I said. "The first loss of an officer in our seventy year history of game and fish business in Tennessee. First officer murdered in the line of duty. I like the idea of me replacing him. I'm alone now…well, there's the dog, but she'll be fine with the move. My daughters are grown. It's just me and that house with all those memories, James. I like the idea of change."

"You know that people will think you've been demoted," he said.

"I don't care," I said.

"I do," he said. "And who will replace you?"

"McEllis is a good man," I said. "He's been my second for eight years. He knows the business. He cares like I do."

"Does he know about this?"

"I tell McEllis pretty much everything."

"Anybody else know?"

"Ella does. She's clairvoyant like that," I said.

"I heard you been drinking a lot lately. That true?" he asked without emotion.

"You ever seen me drunk? Have you ever had a report of alcohol on my breath at work?"

"Nope. Just people who are your friends have mentioned to me that since Jenny's death, you stay by yourself a lot and seem to drink more."

"That's true, James. Again, the change might help."

He stood and walked to the window, rubbing the back of his head. "I hate this." He turned and crossed his arms. "You see, I don't know whether to be your boss or your friend. Can't see a way to be both."

"Yes, you can. Approve the transfer. My pay will be cut to top officer pay. Let the rumors fly. I don't care so long as you know the truth."

"Big mistake, Ethan. You should never go backwards in your career. It's a rule."

"I have a rule," I said. "Never let your advancing career interfere with your sleep."

He sighed. He looked out his window and sighed again.

"Know this. I think it's a crazy notion. So sleep on it tonight and we'll talk tomorrow."

"Like I said, I don't sleep," I said.

"Then roll around and ponder all night. I don't care. Just wait a day," he said.

"You think this is the first day I've hatched this idea? My mind is made up," I said.

James sighed again. "I'll appoint McEllis as acting chief for one year. After that, if things don't work out like you think, you come back. Agreed?"

"Agreed," I said. "One year."

"We have another problem," he said.

"What?"

"You can't stand your new boss," he said. "And for good reason. Benny is a trouble-maker and I should have never allowed his promotion. Y'all will fight from day one."

I smiled. "No, he will not be a problem. And besides, there are some good officers in that area. I've known W.B. for fifteen years."

"W.B. Langford. Now there's a hard case. That man scares the hell out of me."

"He's a real good man, if he likes you. Real dangerous if he doesn't," I said. "We've always been close."

"When do you want to do this?" he asked.

I stood and moved to the door. "Today would be nice," I said. "I hate putting things off."

James looked out the window. "Okay, I'll call personnel and get the paperwork started and notify the regional manager."

"Thanks, James."

"And Ethan, it's not the job that's causing your sleep problem." he said. "Just so we're straight on that."

I smiled and left his office, contemplating the most scenic route to Houston County. And for the first time in years, I was scared.

Living on a hundred acre lake has its advantages. Jenny and I built the house so we could fish and swim whenever we felt the urge. The main advantage, we learned, is not the fishing or swimming, however. The view of the water is the thing. I have always pondered the soothing effect of water on the soul, but haven't determined its medicating abilities yet. Can't figure that one out, but it's real. Maybe the sight and sound of the flowing creek in Houston County will suffice. So at dusk, I sat at the water's edge with the ugly dog, watching the lake move with its reflective light and life of its own. The whiskey was strong in the glass and I felt its effects. The dog lay at my feet, her hair still wet from the earlier retrieves. Tomorrow, I would go to Houston County and find Taylor James, but tonight I would stay out of the house as long as possible.

Later, after one more drink, the moonlight changed the water's appearance. Its personality is softer at night, more sensual. I stared into it…

"The water hasn't chilled yet, you know," she said.
"You think?" I said.
"I do."
"You first."

She moved from the chair, pulling her shirt over her head. She discarded her shorts on the dock and paused with the sparkling water behind her silhouette, then turned and smiled, before diving into the water with barely a splash. She silently surfaced.

"Well," I said.

"It's great," she said. "Come here."

"You lie, gotta be cold."

"Don't make me come get you," she said.

"Please, come get me."

She swam toward me and rose from the water, standing naked in the moonlight.

It was two in the morning when I awoke, lying on the grass at the water's edge, my dog curled against me like a lover. I looked quickly toward the water, but Jenny was not there. Even sober, I could not leave the water's edge…not until the first light chased away all chances that she would reappear.

CHAPTER 2

I headed east on I-40 the next morning at daylight, crossing the Caney Fork River five times before turning north toward the little town of Red Boiling Springs around nine. I dialed her number.

"Hello."

"Mrs. Johnson?"

"Yes."

"This is Ethan Stewart. I worked with Samuel. Is Amanda there?"

"Why, yes. I'll get her."

I drove a half a mile.

"Hello."

"Amanda, this is Ethan."

"Ethan. How are you?" she said quickly.

"I'm fine," I said. "Could I see you this morning?"

"Well, yes. Where are you?"

"About thirty minutes out."

"Do you remember where my parents live?"

"Yes. I do. I won't stay long. I just need to see you because I'm moving tomorrow and it may be a while before I can see you again."

"Where are you going, Ethan?"

"I'll be there shortly," I said.

She was sitting on the front porch when I arrived. Todd, the younger boy was sitting with her in the swing. Amanda was a striking, tall girl with a strong jaw and blue eyes. I climbed the porch steps and she stood up. She wore cut off jeans and a faded UT sweatshirt. She was crying before I could hug her.

"It's okay," I said.

"I'm sorry," she said. "Just the sight of any of his friends still makes me cry."

She returned to the swing and Mrs. Johnson came to the front door. "Mom, would you take Todd in, please?"

I stood and shook the older lady's hand. She wore an apron that had flour dusted on the front.

"Would you like some coffee, Mr. Stewart?" she said.

"No ma'am. Thanks."

And the grandmother took the young boy by the hand and led him through the front door. Amanda sat in the swing and looked over the farm.

I sat across from her in a rocker. "How are you?"

She looked at me. "How am I supposed to be, Ethan? How were you three months after Jenny died?"

"A mess," I said. "But I didn't show it."

She laughed. "Well, I'm a mess and I show it."

"That's probably better," I said.

"I won't ever get over this," she said. "Samuel was my life. He was the center of everything I lived for."

"You will get over this," I said. "I know you can't see it now, but you will."

"Have you?" she said.

"No," I said. "But I will. I have to. That's why I'm moving to Houston County and taking Samuel's job."

She looked at me with amazement. "You're the Chief. That's crazy!"

"Is it?" I said. "Everybody keeps telling me that, but it seems perfectly logical to me."

"Why, Ethan? Why would you do that?"

"Several reasons," I said. "One is that I believe in what Samuel died for. Second, they can't win or he died for nothing. Third, those people hurt you and I won't tolerate that."

"And they'll kill you, too."

"I guess we'll see about that," I said.

Amanda stopped the swing and moved to a chair next to me. She took my hand. "Listen to me, Ethan. Good people cannot win a war of violence against bad people. You will have to change to stay alive."

"You mean I'll have to be bad, too," I said.

"That's exactly what I mean. Samuel refused and it killed him. You guys think that good law enforcement training can protect you." She laughed. "That's a joke," she said. "You're out there in the middle of nowhere and everybody's got guns and you think being the good guy is gonna protect you.

Well, it didn't, Ethan." She shook her head. "It didn't."

"No, it didn't," I said. "And I'm sorry for that. But he was a good man, and that is the thing. Good men need backup, even when they're gone. I'm his backup, Amanda, and I'm going."

"What are you gonna do, Ethan? You can't fix this."

"Here's what I'm gonna do. That…thing…that killed your husband is going to kneel at your feet and say he's sorry. I will give him a chance to do that. And if I can get him to do that, then you'll be faced with whether you can forgive him or not. I'll give him that chance and I'll give you that chance. And that's the only way I can figure how to do this thing and remain me."

She looked at me and smiled. "You are the only man alive that I would believe could do that. Samuel thought you walked on water. I almost do. So you do that, Ethan. You bring Tiller Mabry to me and let him kneel at my feet. Then see what happens."

"I just wanted you to know before I go." And I stood to leave.

"What happens if he won't come?" she said.

"He'll come or he won't be able to come," I said. "But I'll give him the chance."

She stood and walked to me and took both my hands in hers. "You're a good man, Ethan Stewart. And you've hurt like I hurt now. I've never known a man who loved his wife more than you loved Jenny. Don't do this. Walk away. Find some happiness for the rest of your life and move on."

"It's love. I love Jenny. You said loved. It's love," I said. "And I can't walk away. I've tried. I can't."

And she hugged me real hard and I felt the wetness in her eyes on my shirt and I hugged her back and kissed her head and walked off that porch toward the rest of my life.

CHAPTER 3

I chose to drive my Jeep, not the state vehicle. April offered that pretense of summer in the air and with the top down, I could smell the summer coming. Also, I didn't want everyone to know who I was...not yet anyway.

Leaving I-40 heading north, the country became rural very quickly. Oaks stands and clean pastures gave way to larger stands of oaks the farther I drove. The creeks I crossed were clean and clear running and the traffic was sparse. Once I crossed the Houston County line, solid hardwoods lined the pastures in the hollows, providing a green, fuzzy hue of new leaves. I saw very few row crop acres, but some small tobacco plots. This country was backwoods Tennessee at its best and its isolation from the larger cities had preserved some quality of integrity I found interesting, like looking through an old family album and wishing for times less complicated. Every car or truck I met, the driver waved. Nice…

I used gravel roads to skirt the county seat of Erin and continued west to Kentucky Lake. I wanted to see the house one more time before trying to find Taylor James.

The road was lonely. No vehicles. I remembered all the roads we had explored together. Jenny was great company, always questioning, eyes wide open, seeing everything.

"You are very quiet," she said.

"Just thinking," I said.

Jenny knew the transition from 'just thinking' was too fast. She knew me that well. After all these years, she should. So she didn't pry, but she could have. I tell her most everything. And I'm not afraid. That is what drew us together, I think, so long ago on that campus our senior year. We would stop walking under big trees and talk for hours, lost in our ability to totally say what we felt. No games. No false egos.

I looked at her. "You're scary," I said.

"I'm sexy, too." she smiled.

"Sexier than twenty years ago," I said.

"Don't joke," she said.

"No, it's true. And certainly more skilled," I said.

"Keep it up," she said, "and we'll stop the truck."

I smiled. She was still beautiful. I didn't think that possible when I was thirty. Her body still talked to me. Her magnificent brown eyes still stopped my thoughts. There is something amazingly good about growing older together. I swerved to miss a gray squirrel that dashed across the road, but heard a sickening thump. Looking in the rear view mirror I watched it kick madly before death stilled it.

"Did you hit it?" she asked.

"Nope."

"Good," she said, knowing I was lying, but refusing to acknowledge animals hit by our vehicles. Thirty years of marriage develops strange habits...all for the sake of less pain.

The Jeep bounced when I crossed Cooley Ford Bridge; I looked over the bridge rails. I could see three kids playing in a deep blue pool of water. Their backs were sunburned, but their legs were very white, contrasting markedly with carefully planned urban tans. I bet the water was still winter cold. I turned west following the gravel road for another mile before seeing the faded dirt road that led to the house. In its front yard, I stopped, shut down the Jeep engine, got out and stretched my legs.

The house was of original log construction, the logs wide, maybe eighteen inches of yellow poplar. The porch extended on three sides and was massive, with limestone slabs as porch steps. Sitting on the hill among the oaks, the house immediately impressed me again as a place one could rest in peace. Ugly Dog would love the place...

White Oak Creek ran off to the side, clearly visible from the porch, with its sun-glittering shoals and deep blue pools. I saw no other humans. No street lights. I heard no cars...and then I heard popping gravel behind me.

A new black Ford truck pulled in behind the Jeep. The driver stared at me for a second, and then with purpose, got out. She wore faded jeans and scarred roper boots and a green sweatshirt with KODIAK stamped in white letters. She wasn't smiling. A big yellow lab followed her and walked at heel until she stopped and then it sat obediently. Well trained.

"May I help you?" she said.

"I hope so," I said.

Her eyes found the badge clipped on my belt and I suppose she saw the grips of the 1911 that were visible under my vest.

"You're not from around here," she said.

"No ma'am. I'm new, but I'm hoping you are Miss Taylor James."

"I am."

"I'm Ethan Stewart. I'll be replacing Samuel Dooley as the wildlife officer for this county," I said, extending my hand. She took it and the handshake was firm. All business. The dog watched me.

"Where's your green truck?"

"Sometimes, I drive my personal vehicle," I said.

"Where's your uniform?"

"In my closet. I hate them," I said. "Who's your friend?"

"That's Jasper," she said. She paused. "I'm sorry about Samuel," she said. "He was a great guy."

"Yes, he was," I said.

She looked up at me for the first time, eyes to eyes, and hers were a deep brown with lighter golden flakes. "So, how can I help you, Mr. Stewart?"

"It's Ethan," I said."

She sort of smiled. "How can I help you?" she said again.

"Is this your house?" I asked.

"Yes," she said. "It was my father's get-away cabin before he passed away."

I leaned against the Jeep and removed a thermos. "Care for some coffee?"

"No thanks," she said.

"Would it be possible for us to move to the porch and sit down?" I asked.

"Sure," she said, and we climbed the rock steps to the porch and sat at a primitive wooden table with two chairs. The dog never left her side.

"What was he getting away from?" I asked.

"I'm sorry," she said.

"Your dad. You said it was his get-away cabin."

"Oh, probably all the girls in the house. Mom and me and my sister."

"I see," I said, watching her nervously play with her key chain on the table. Her fingernails were clean, but non-manicured and attractively short. The back of her hands were tan and I noticed two small scars. No wedding ring, but a wide silver band on her right hand.

"I have two daughters," I said. "I understand your father's position, but it doesn't mean he didn't love you," I said.

She looked up and smiled, genuinely for the first time. "He loved us a lot," she said. "So, Mr. Stewart, when did you move here?"

"It's Ethan. It's 'So, Ethan, when did you move?"

She smiled. "When did you move?"

"I haven't yet. I'm looking for a place to buy. It has to be on a hill. It has to have oaks in the yard. It has to be next to a beautiful creek. It has to be close to the lake."

"So you are very particular," she said.

"Very," I said. "To a fault."

"This house is not for sale," she said.

"I heard that," I said.

"Then why did you come?" she asked.

"Curious," I said. "I've learned that things can change when you least expect it. Even when the sun is out and there's no cloud in the sky, there's always a chance of rain."

She got up and moved to the porch rail. "My daddy said the best law enforcement we could have out here is a good game warden. He thought you guys were more stable than local law enforcement."

"I think I would have liked your father," I said.

She leaned against the rail. "You are older than I would have thought Samuel's replacement to be."

I paused. "I asked to come here. I like this country."

"From where?" she asked.

"Around Nashville," I said.

"Why?" she asked.

"Why what?"

"Why did you want to move? A man your age generally has his life in order and change isn't something he wants."

I smiled at her. "What is KODIAK?" I asked.

"The Alaska KODIAK."

"Ever been there?" I asked.

"Several times," she said. "Does that surprise you?"

"Honestly?" I asked.

"Honestly," she said.

"Yes."

"Why?"

"I'm not sure," I said. "Where do you live?"

She pointed behind the cabin. "That way about a quarter mile. I live in the home place. There's a path from the back of this cabin to my house. Daddy walked it whenever he needed to escape."

"Your mother?" I asked.

"She moved to Nashville after Daddy died. Said she wasn't staying out here without him."

"But you stayed," I said."

"I'm not going anywhere," she said.

"And your sister," I asked.

"She's married and a mom, living in Knoxville."

"I see," I said.

She looked me straight in the eyes. "I know this. You're no ordinary game warden," she said. "And you seem awful nosy."

"No ma'am. I'm not," I said.

"You're not what? Nosy or a normal game warden?"

"Neither of those things," I said.

And her cell phone rang. She looked at the number and answered, moving away from me on the porch. Jasper followed. "Calm down," she said. And then listened some more. "Where are you?" Listened some more. "How fast can you get here?" Pause. "Come to Daddy's cabin." And she hung up. When she looked up there was a different look on her face.

"Sure you don't want some coffee," I asked. "Made it myself and I make real good coffee."

"No, I'm good," she said. "But you need to leave or be prepared for a situation."

"I love situations," I said.

She moved to the front door of the cabin, unlocked it, and emerged with a Remington 870, and racked a shell into the chamber. I heard the safety click on. She sat at the table, the gun across her lap.

"I have a young cousin named Julia. She's eighteen and a spitfire. We're more like sisters than cousins, even though she's many years younger than me." She paused. "There are some violent people in this county as you already know and one particular family...the Mabrys, who I know you have heard of. One of the Mabry clan is about twenty, and really mean, and he has always had a thing for Julia, who wouldn't give him the time of day. He just stopped her on the road about five miles from here. He wouldn't let her leave, so she shot him with pepper spray and now he's chasing her...coming here."

I smiled. "Wow," I said. "Always this exciting around here?"

"We have our moments," she said.

"Why did she call you?" I asked.

"Cause I have a shotgun and she trusts me."

"Wow," I said again. I stood and looked down the road, evaluating the cover. "Will you do what I say?" I asked.

"Sure, to a point," she said.

"What's that point?" I asked.

"I won't let that bastard hurt Julia or me or you or my dog," she said. "That's a promise."

"I believe you," I said. "I'm going to ease over in those woods and get behind him. He will see you on the porch with the gun. Get Julia on the porch with you quickly. When I announce myself, he will turn to me. Keep the gun on him while we talk. I'll take care of everything from there. Okay, Taylor?"

"Why do you want me to hold the gun on him while you talk?" she asked.

"That's simple. If he shoots me…kill him," I said as I moved off the porch into the woods. I stopped and turned back to her. "Do you mind me calling you Taylor?" I asked.

"Are you not just a little nervous?" she said shaking her head.

"Sure," I said. "Feels great." And I disappeared from her view into the dense understory along the road.

Within a minute, an old Chevy truck sped toward the house. Spike Mabry was one hundred yards behind in a jacked-up four-wheel drive Toyota. Julia got out of the first truck and I heard Taylor yell to her and the young girl ran toward the porch. Spike got out of the Toyota in a cloud of dust, took three running steps toward Julia when he saw Taylor on the porch with the Remington. He immediately returned to the Toyota and pulled a .30 caliber carbine from behind the seat and started walking toward the girls. I stepped out ten yards behind him and followed, matching my steps with his.

"That gun don't scare me none!" he yelled to Taylor.

"Shows how stupid you are!" she returned.

"Nobody sprays that shit in my eyes!" he yelled.

"Wanna bet?" I said, three steps behind him.

He swirled around quickly and I saw his left eye swollen and red from the pepper spray. "Who the fuck are you?" he said.

I took one step to the right, toward his bad eye. "A game warden," I said. "Understand… if you move the barrel of that carbine one inch in my direction, I'm going to kill you." My right hand rested on the grips of the 1911.

"You think you're that fast?" he smiled.

I looked up at him. He was a big boy, even with his eye watering. "Can't ever tell, but if you can't shoot me in under four tenths of a second, I'll guarantee you, I'm that fast," I said.

He thought about that. "I don't guess you've heard what we do to game wardens round here," he said.

Stay calm. "Haven't heard," I said. "Why don't you tell me what you do to game wardens around here?"

He smiled. His teeth were dirty. "They seem to get dead," he said.

"How do they get dead?" I asked

"Last one got shot, I heard," he said. "Gut shot and then one to the head."

"So why don't you shoot me?" I asked. "Try it. See what happens," I said.

He stared at my hand. *Indecision.* "Here's what you're gonna do," I said. "Take your right hand off the gun and hold it by the barrel with your left hand and place it on the ground. Do it right now," I said.

He slowly lowered the gun to the ground and stood up. Then he smiled real big. "I'd just as soon whup your ass the old fashioned way, anyway," he said.

I smiled back at him. "Okay, but before you try, let me explain how I have to work. I can't just haul off and kick your ass, even though you deserve it. I have to treat you in what we call the force continuum. Ever heard of that?"

"Huh?"

"See, you just threatened me, so you jumped about four levels and now I can go one step beyond your threat." I quickly walked up to him and hit him open-handed on the side of his right ear….hard. He staggered to his left and I grabbed his left arm, digging my fingers into the radial nerve. He yelled in pain.

"Don't move," I said. "Cause that's called defensive resistance which means I get to slap you again."

He tried to jerk away and I slapped him again on the same ear…harder. He went down. I crouched down in front of him. "Listen to me, Dumbo. You've been pepper sprayed by a girl and bitch-slapped twice by a game warden. Don't you think it smart to just get up and do what I say? If you stay stupid, I get to keep hurting you, which between me and you, I really enjoy," I whispered.

The girls were now standing close to us…watching. Taylor still had the shotgun and Julia stood to her side.

Spike shakily got up and faced me as I stood. He looked at Julia and smirked. "You think this is real funny, don't you, Bitch?"

I slapped him again in the same ear, while he looked at Julia. "That was for bad manners," I said.

"Okay…Okay," he said as he recovered. "What do you want me to do?" he said.

"I'm going to handcuff you for your safety and mine, so I can question you. Do you understand?"

"Yeah," he mumbled. "But I ain't telling you shit. And you can't make me. I want a lawyer."

"Go get one, but I'm still going to ask you some questions."

"You gotta shut up when I ask for a lawyer. That's the law," he said.

"Really," I said. "I'm interviewing you, not interrogating you and I haven't placed you under arrest. So I can ask you anything I want and you can tell me anything you want. You see, we can be real cozy," I said.

"You can kiss my cozy ass," he slurred.

"Turn around and get on your knees," I said.

He did.

"Cross your legs, one foot over the other."

He did.

"Place your hands behind your back and lock your fingers."

He did. I placed my left hand around his thumbs and in the same instant he jerked away. I simply pushed forward on his back and his face slammed into the gravel, completely off balance. That did it. He changed personality in an instant, got to his feet and charged. I stepped to his bad eye as he began a round house swing, drew back my right fist, and struck him with a left forearm to the brachial nerve on the left side of his neck. He immediately collapsed. He tried to get up but his muscles wouldn't work right, so he fell three times trying. The girls backed away, keeping a safe distance. I walked to him. "What'd you hit me with?" he mumbled.

"Stay down and roll over," I said.

He did.

"Put your hands behind your back."

He did. "I'm done," he whispered. "Can't move right."

I cuffed him and stood him up on wobbly legs. "Now," I said. "You are under arrest for assaulting an officer."

"You gonna read me my rights now, I bet," he said.

"I watched you assault me, Big Boy. I don't need to talk to you." I collected the carbine, unloaded it, and walked him to the Jeep, where I placed him in the front seat and fastened the seat belt. "Be good," I said. "Or I'll slap you again."

"Miss Julia, would you come here?" I asked.

Taylor and Julia moved to the Jeep, along with Jasper who was now seriously watching Spike.

"Apologize to her," I said to Spike.

He just looked at me. "Apologize," I said.

He looked at her. "Sorry," he mumbled.

I leaned over and whispered in his good ear. "And if you or any of your family ever even look at her or Miss James again, I'll find you and break your filthy neck," I said.

He nodded.

I walked the girls to the porch steps. "Miss Julia," I said. "I will need to interview you regarding the incident later."

She smiled and extended her hand. "Who are you?" she asked.

"I'm the man who wants to live in this house," I said, shaking her hand. "If you have any influence on Miss James, I'd appreciate a good word." I turned to Taylor. "This is kind of embarrassing, but I need directions to the jail."

"Right downtown Erin," she said. "Behind the courthouse on the hill."

"Thanks. I'll call a wrecker from the jail and have his truck towed."

"Are you going back to Nashville tonight?" she asked.

"Depends," I said. "This will take a couple of hours."

"Come back. This is my guest house. You can stay here tonight. We'll cook something on the grill and finish our conversation."

I looked up. "Not a cloud in the sky," I said. "I'll be back…."

CHAPTER 4

Somewhere around four in the afternoon, I returned to the log house. I had processed my prisoner without incident, although the deputies looked surprised that Spike Mabry sat handcuffed in my Jeep. They were professionally friendly, but lacked the brotherly attitude I was accustomed to. I had asked to see the sheriff, but he was unavailable. Spike told me one more time to kiss his ass before I left the jail. I smiled and asked him to please have a nice day.

I climbed the steps of the house and saw a note taped to the front door. It read, "Door's open. If you need a drink, the whisky is on the bar. I suspect you deserve one. Call me at 289-3101 when you're hungry…..Taylor."

I opened the door and stepped inside. Clean. The den was large and rustic. The furniture was Appalachian primitive. The floor was dark hardwood with a large rug next to a massive fireplace. One entire wall was a constructed bookshelf and it was full. I perused the titles. All my favorites….Hemingway, Ruark, Dennison, McCarthy, Roosevelt, and Leopold were there. And many more. I liked the man already. Duck calls hung from picture frames that displayed many of David Wright's paintings. And wingbone turkey calls that I could tell were used, not just for display. I looked at the floor in front of the door and there were scratches representing some family dog of the past. The house smelled of old wood and fireplace dampness.

On the bar were several bottles of brown whiskey. Jack Daniels and Knob Creek and Jim Beam. There were two glasses on the bar and I took one and headed for the refrigerator. Ice was in trays, so I emptied one and refilled it from the faucet. I tasted the water and smiled. I had not tasted water of that purity in a long while. I bet there's a springhouse out back. I poured a half glass of Knob Creek over ice and let it settle, as I moved from the kitchen to the rest of the house.

A staircase going to the second floor was in the back of the den and a door leading to the master bedroom. The bedroom was spacious and a huge bathroom adjoined it. The head of the bed was constructed of chestnut boards fifteen inches wide, probably sawed in the late eighteen hundreds. Old quilts on the bed.

There was a large mud room to the side and out back was a deck with the grill. Behind the deck, across the yard was the spring house, a small log structure with a front door. I leaned against the deck rail and took the first sip. It burned smoothly. I could see a faint foot-trail behind the springhouse leading through the hardwoods to Taylor James. *I wonder what she is doing right now.* I tried to recall her face. Clear, brown eyes…light brown hair…small, white scar at the corner of her mouth.

Crickets voiced at the yard's edge and I tried to remember the formula for determining the temperature by counting chirps and dividing by some abstract number. I used to know…

I walked through the yard toward the springhouse and looked back. I pictured the house in snow with smoke rising from the chimney. I wouldn't sell this house either.

I opened my cell phone and dialed the number. It rang three times and she answered.

"I'm back," I said.

"Good," she said. "Everything all right?"

"Yes ma'am. No problems. I admire your father's taste in whiskey, by the way," I said.

"That's my whiskey," she said. "Daddy never drank."

"Then I admire your taste in whiskey," I said.

"Can you cook?" she asked.

"When I'm forced," I said.

"Then consider yourself forced," she said. "It's not that I can't cook. I just hate it," she said.

"What should I cook?"

"I bring the meat. You cook it. Will that work?" she asked.

"How fast can you get here?" I asked. "I'm hungry."

"I'm on the way," she said, and hung up.

When she arrived I was on the front porch still nursing the first drink. She smiled getting out of the truck…still in jeans, but a different top, with autumn colors swirled in an abstract pattern. Jasper was with her again. I moved to the steps.

"What do you think of the house?" she asked handing me a sack of food.

"Honestly?" I asked.

"Yes," she said.

"I wouldn't sell it either," I said, reaching down and patting the yellow dog, who liked my attention.

"Hmm," she said entering the front door.

"What does hmmm mean?" I asked.

She went to the bar and retrieved the other glass. "Jasper likes you. That doesn't happen often."

"There's ice in a bowl in the refrigerator," I said. "And I filled up the tray, in case you're wondering. And dogs always like me."

She turned and looked at me. "I wasn't wondering if you were responsible," she said. "I know you are. And the ice is in the freezer."

"Well, the ice is in the big, white box thing in the kitchen. And how do you know I'm responsible?"

She poured her drink, selecting Knob Creek too, I noticed. "Some secretary named Ella in your Nashville office told me. We had a nice talk."

I was taken aback. I took another drink. "It's impossible to have a nice conversation with Ella," I said. "It's always banter. And why did you call Nashville?"

"Some man shows up at my doorstep wanting to buy my father's house and he's no ordinary game warden, by his own admission, I might add, and he handles a very violent situation like it's an entertaining training drill, and instantly makes himself enemy to the most dangerous family in this county, so I call the main office to ask a few questions," she said. "Isn't that reasonable, Chief?"

I paused at the chief word. "Unexpected, but very reasonable," I said. "And what did Ella say?"

"Well, she is very discreet. But I did find out that you have been Chief of Law Enforcement for ten years and that if anyone did anything to hurt you while you were temporarily insane, she would personally come down here and cut their heads off," she said smiling.

I scooted around Taylor in the kitchen, added ice and freshened my drink. She smelled fresh, soap and a hint of some perfume I could not define. Just a breath of a hint. Nice. "And she would, too," I said.

"She also told me, when I asked for a reference regarding the house, that you were the finest man she had ever known," she said.

"Hmmm," I said.

"So, are you two having an affair?" she asked.

"I asked her," I said smiling. "She said no."

Taylor looked away briefly, hiding a smile. "Ella also asked for my cup size. Said it would be real impressive if she could provide you with that," she said laughing for the first time.

Ouch. "I guess you had to be there to understand," I said. "When I ask her to acquire information for me, she always tries to get more than I asked. Did she ask if you played guitar?"

She looked perplexed. "No."

"Do you?" I asked.

"No. Took piano lessons once cause my momma demanded it. Hated it," she said. "Why?"

"Do you sing?" I asked.

"Never," she said. "Not even when I've been drinking. Again, why?"

I smiled. "Taylor James. James Taylor. You know. It was a bet we had about you. And she lost."

"My parents were big fans," she said.

"And you?"

"He's great. When I'm in that introspective, wondering about life, kinda mood. Do you like him?"

I took a drink and smiled. "Yes," I said. "When I'm in that introspective, wondering about life mood."

"And how often is that?"

"Quite a long, long time," I said. "And I feel fine."

She smiled at me, knowing there was some meaning there, but she couldn't quite find the lyrics in her memory. She moved to the table and sat, swirling her whiskey in ice. "So, are you temporarily insane?" she asked. "Coming to backwoods Tennessee to live and catch bad guys."

I took a seat across from her at the table. Her eyes watched me prepare for the answer. "If it's insane to leave a position of influence and power to find some relic of happiness, then maybe I am. What do you think?"

She tasted the whiskey. "I think it's brave," she said seriously. "But very unusual, because most men believe their happiness is influence and power."

"My happiness seems to be elusive," I said. We were quiet for a moment. "What did 'hmmm' mean?"

"When?"

"I said, 'I wouldn't sell the house either,' and you said "hmmm."

"You don't forget anything, do you?" she said.

"Yeah…birthdays and stuff," I said.

"It surprised me. That's all," she said. "If you really wanted this house, that wasn't the best sales pitch. And it surprised me that Jasper took to you so quick."

"It's the truth, though," I said. "The truth rarely sells anything except itself."

"Sometimes, that's enough," she said. "So you never asked for my cup size?"

"No ma'am. It never crossed my mind."

She smiled again. "You going to cook or not?" she added quickly.

"Sure," I said. "Where's the charcoal, or do I build a fire the old way."

"Charcoal is in a storage box on the deck. I'll start the potatoes."

"I thought you didn't cook," I said.

"Baking a potato is hardly cooking," she said. "And neither is throwing lettuce in a bowl."

"How do you like your steak?" I asked.

"Medium. No blood, but pink."

"That is medium," I said. "No blood and pink."

"So now we both know we both know and I won't be disappointed in my supper, "she said.

I raised an eyebrow and smiled. "Yes, ma'am." I turned and almost made it outside.

"Will your wife like the house?" she said loudly so I could hear.

I stopped, looked back at her and paused.

"The ring," she said.

"She would have loved the house," I said. And I walked outside and shut the door.

It was almost dark when she brought the steaks outside on a platter. I was sitting in an old wooden chair watching the glowing coals. A barred owl called by the creek and another answered nearby. She pulled up a chair and sat next to me. We didn't say anything for a long time.

"My wife died last year and so she won't be coming."

"I'm sorry," she said finally.

I looked at her through the half light. "Yeah, me, too," I said. I moved to the grill and stirred the coals and then threw on the meat. It sizzled on the hot steel and the aroma filled the air around us.

"Why do you like the house?" she asked.

"Lots of reasons," I said. "The location is perfect, but also, do you have any idea how big the trees were that these logs were made from?"

"No," she said. "Never thought about it."

"These logs had to come from the heart of the tree to get that width and the trees had to be over one hundred feet tall. Imagine a yellow poplar stand with trees that tall."

"And that means something to you?" she asked.

"Yeah, it'll never happen again. And that's sad."

"That's interesting. That you would find that sad. Anything else?" she asked.

"I seem to like my neighbor," I said. "First impression, anyway."

"Why?"

"She's smart. She's got grit. Great taste in whiskey. Will guarantee she turns heads in a crowded room. And she grabs a shotgun when things get serious."

"Most men would find that intimidating," she said.

"Not me," I said. "I like it."

"Anything else?" she asked, without giving any clue as to her feelings about the compliments.

"Yeah, I can talk to her the first day I meet her like I've trusted her for years, even if she didn't stay very long at the table."

"What?"

"You moved. You sat at the table and then I sat at the table and then you moved."

"And that means something to you?"

"Maybe. Maybe not. But it was interesting."

"Why?"

"I don't know," I said. "Help me out? Are we talking why it's easy to talk to you or why you moved from the table?"

She smiled and finished her drink. "Hmmm," she said. "And where am I sitting now? How long have I been here? Kinda blows your 'maybe' theory, huh? Don't burn the steaks." And she went back inside the house.

The steaks were perfect. The potatoes were undercooked, and she never apologized. I found coffee and made half a pot. It smelled good in the room, but she refused to drink it.

"You don't wear a ring," I said.

"Nope," she said. "It's down in the creek if you care to look some day. Probably buy yourself a new Jeep with what it's worth.

"I see," I said. "Not still friends, I take it."

"Oh, no," she said.

"Anybody now?" I asked.

"Yes. We've been seeing each other for a year, I guess. He lives in Clarksville. Sells real estate."

"Why doesn't he live here?" I asked.

"Because I haven't asked him," she said.

"And you won't go there?"

She looked at me and frowned. "I told you. I'm not going anywhere."

"What's his name?"

"Tom. His name is Tom."

"It's no good, you know," I said.

"What?"

I thought before speaking. "Nothing."

"Oh no," she said. "Can't do that. Nothing always means something interesting."

I paused. "For me," I started. "If it's not right, it's not right and there's no sense in wasting time with 'not right'."

She smiled. "So, you don't believe in things working out over time, even when they don't start out exactly right?"

"No ma'am. I don't."

"Most men find it difficult to talk to me," she said. "So rarely would it start out 'just right' with me. I have to be patient."

"I can see why most men have a problem talking to you. You're tough."

"Doesn't seem to scare you," she said.

"That's cause I'm tough, too."

"I've been with tough men before, Chief. They still couldn't talk to me."

I smiled. "I would appreciate it if you didn't call me Chief."

She raised her eyebrow.

"I didn't mean tough as a face-smashing kind of thing," I said.

"What did you mean?"

"Maybe brave enough to trust yourself to talk," I said. "We may be kindred spirits."

"You believe in kindred spirits?" she asked.

"Absolutely," I said.

She went to the sink and began stacking dishes. She spoke without looking at me. "I'll rent you the house for a month, but nothing leaves the house. It stays exactly the same as it is now. At the end of a month, we'll talk again and see if we'll go six months. If you've still here after a year, we'll talk about a purchase," she said. She turned to look at me.

"So, we won't talk for a month?" I asked.

"About the house," she said.

"Oh, you said, 'We'll talk again in a month,' and I thought...."

"I know what I said," she said. "I was talking about the house."

"So we can talk, like every day, if we wanted," I said.

"If we wanted," she said.

"You think I could bring some things, like clothes and guns and books," I asked.

"Sure," she said.

"You said, 'The house stays exactly the same,' and I just want to make sure we both know what 'medium' means."

"You like to argue, don't you?"

"No, I don't. But I hate misunderstandings. I also have a dog."

"What breed?" she asked.

"Deutsch Drahthaar," I said.

"What?" she asked.

"Easier to call them DDs. Not so common a breed," I said.

"What do they look like? What do they do?"

"Ugly dogs, unless you love them. And they do everything...point, retrieve, blood trail, track."

She smiled. "Maybe it will get along with Jasper."

"Berit gets along with everybody, except snakes. She's a snake killing machine." I said.

"You haven't asked 'how much?'"

"Okay, how much?"

"What do you think is fair?" she asked.

"My daddy told me to never price another man's gun," I said.

"Okay," she said. "Eight hundred a month."

"In Houston County?" I said. "How bout I pay nothing and guarantee your farm poacher-free while I'm here."

She laughed out loud for the first time. Her teeth were very white. "Okay, how about four hundred a month and if you're still here in a year, the total amount will go toward the purchase price."

"That's a good deal, so long as you don't inflate the purchase price," I said. "Perhaps we should agree on the purchase price before." I smiled and extended my hand.

She took it and we shook. "Handshake deal. No contract," she said. She pulled a house key from her rear jean pocket and handed it to me.

"You have my word," I said.

"And you have mine," she said.

She started toward the door. "I've got to go. Sleep well," she said.

"Thanks for the steak and good conversation," I said. "It's been a very good day, and it's been awhile since I've said that."

She paused at the door and turned, leaning against the log wall looking back at me. "Just so we're clear," she began. "I don't pretend to believe what my intuition says about you," she finished.

"What does your intuition say?" I asked.

"That you are a good man," she said.

"I won't ever lie to you," I said. "But other than that, I'm still working on the good part."

"Well, you are different than any man I've ever known for one day, and don't ask me to explain that, but know this, Spike Mabry's hurt good men around here and he's not half as bad as his big brother."

"Spike Mabry is big and strong and stupid and very dangerous," I said. "I know that."

"His brother is not so big, and not so strong, and very, very, smart," she warned. "And he will absolutely kill you."

"You mean, Tiller Mabry?" I said.

"Yes."

"So, I've heard," I said and then we didn't speak for an uncomfortable time. "I enjoyed your company, Taylor."

She smiled. "It was nice," she said before moving through the front door. She turned on the porch and looked back. "I didn't plan to move from the table. I wasn't even aware I did it, until you mentioned it. You don't scare me. And I think you think too much." And she went down the steps to her truck, her dog, Jasper, at heel.

I moved to the open door and then to the porch rail. "I would like to know what music is in your CD player right now," I asked.

She stopped. "Are you serious?" she asked.

"Yes," I said.

"Why?" she asked.

"I wonder, that's all," I said.

"Guess," she said.

"I will not," I said smiling. "Guessing would ruin it."

"Telling would ruin it," she said.

She opened the door, got in, and started the truck. I saw the window roll down. Suddenly, Jimmy Buffet spilled into the night, as she turned the player up loud. And I heard Cheeseburger in Paradise until her taillights disappeared in the darkness.

CHAPTER 5

I slept. All night. The window's morning light was my first vision. I lay there trying to remember my last full night of sleep. Not since before Jenny died. A year. I could feel the coolness of late spring through the open window and I didn't want to move, so I shut my eyes.

My cell phone rang on the bedside table. I looked at my watch…6:30. I looked at the number…Ella. I fumbled for the phone and opened it.

"Hello, Bucket Mouth," I whispered.

"I swear I didn't know it was her, Ethan, until after a few questions," she said. "She is very good… and did you just call me 'Bucket Mouth'?"

"I did," I said. "With respect. I heard it in a movie. Costner was disappointed at Duvall for giving away trusted information and at this early hour, it seems to be the same thing."

"I'm not Robert damned Duvall," she said. "And you sure aren't Kevin Costner."

"They really cared for each other," I said. "I mean in the movie…in a manly way, nothing gay or anything. Bucket Mouth doesn't mean I don't love you," I said.

"Well, when I say you've lost your mind and you are an absolute idiot for leaving Chiefdom, that doesn't mean I don't still love you," she said.

"She asked if we were having an affair," I said.

"Who?"

"Taylor James," I said.

"And you said?"

"That I didn't want to, but you forced me."

"Y'all are moving pretty fast," she said. "You've known her, what, fifteen hours?"

"Help me out…what kind of woman listens to Jimmy Buffet?" I asked.

"I listen to Jimmy Buffet," she said.

"You do?"

"I do."

"Well, I don't, so help me out?"

"She dreams of easy times with no stress," she said. "Barefoot and sun and rum. That's what Buffet does for me."

"I see," I said.

"What's she like?" she said.

"I enjoyed being with her," I said. "That's all I know."

She paused. "Be careful, Ethan. You're scaring me a bit."

"I'm scared," I said. "So what's up?"

"I found W.B and he said he would call. I gave him your secret number."

"Thanks," I said. "I'll see you soon."

"I'm serious, Ethan. Go slow. Be your serious, calculating self," she said.

I got up, made coffee and got dressed. In that order. I was at the front door in twenty minutes and stopped because I caught a faint scent of her. I leaned closer to the log where her head had rested. Nothing.

I had been on the road for twenty minutes when W. B. called. "Where are you?" he asked without a hello.

"Headed your way," I said.

"Meet me at Yellow Creek...the little store there."

"Ten-four," I said.

When I arrived twenty minutes later, W.B was standing at his truck drinking coffee from a dented Stanley thermos cup. He walked to the Jeep and got in, all six foot, six inches of him. He put out his hand, and I took it.

"How ya been?" he asked.

"I'll make it a while longer, I reckon," I said.

"Ya never know," he said.

"I appreciate you helping me out. I need a driver to get all the vehicles moved," I said.

"No problem," he said. "We need to talk, anyway. Lots of rumors floatin' around, I guess you know.

"Already?"

"From the mountains of east Tennessee to the Mississippi River, the game warden grape vine is a hummin' with rumors of Ethan Stewart getting demoted, and his punishment is Houston County," he said.

"Punishment for what?" I asked.

"Nobody knows...some say drinkin' on the job."

I looked at him and smiled. "This is a good thing, W.B.," I said.

He looked at me. "What're you up to?" he yelled over the wind noise of the open-topped Jeep.

"Nothing," I said. "Just wanna be a game warden again. That's all."

"Whatever," he said. And we didn't say another word for thirty minutes.

"I've got a cancer," he said loudly.

I looked at him and then back at the road. I pulled over and stopped. "What?"

"Lungs, they say."

"How far along? I mean, how bad?"

"Bad's relative, I reckon," he said. "But six months is what they're giving me without any treatment."

"And with treatment?"

"Six months. They say it will be easier," he said.

"And you say?" I asked.

"Fuck em, is what I say. No treatment for me."

"I'm sorry, W.B.," I said wishing there were better words.

"Everybody's gonna die, Ethan. I've lived a lot longer than I planned to," he said.

"You aren't dead yet," I said. "You never can tell about things."

"Yeah," he said in his deep voice. I can tell you about one thing. I'm gonna kill that son of a bitch, Tiller Mabry for murderin' that kid. That's my good-bye present to his sweet wife and kids."

I looked at him as he lighted a cigarette. Now, I had a big problem. In the years I had known the man, I never once doubted his word. If he said it, it happened. Period. I had never seen any man, or three that could control W.B. physically. He was the best pistol shot, rifleman, and shotgun handler in west Tennessee. A decorated war veteran. A confirmed bachelor. No family. And the most dangerous, honorable man I had ever known.

"Thanks a lot for telling me," I said. "Now, I'm in this. I now have information about a felony that may take place and I am an accomplice, if I don't stop you."

"That's funny," he said laughing for the first time.

"What?"

"That you could stop me," he said.

I looked at him seriously. "It's not funny to me," I said.

"I had my reasons for tellin' you," he said. "You kinda messed everything up with this transfer of yours. I'm tryin' to be your friend. When Tiller dies, and I guaran-damn-tee he will die, they may blame you cause you and me think alike sometimes, so you remember I said it."

"That doesn't solve my problem of knowledge before the fact," I said.

"Oh," he smiled. "That's easy. Hell, I was just funnin' you, Stewart. Can't you take a joke?" And he slapped me on the shoulder. "Tell 'em you thought I was just jokin'. That is if you're dumb enough to ever say we had this conversation. Let's get the hell out of here." And he looked straight ahead while I started the Jeep and pulled away.

I drove twenty miles and not another word was said. I looked across the space between us and he never looked back, so I pulled over and stopped again.

"Get out," I said.

"What for?"

"Just get out."

He obliged me and stretched. I walked around to his side of the vehicle, while he started another smoke.

"What if I told you I had a plan," I said.

"You've always got plans, Ethan. That's why they made you Chief," he said.

"Promise me, you won't do anything until you hear me out," I said.

"When?" he asked, flicking his ashes. "It's not like I have a lot of time."

"Well, not now on the side of the road," I said.

"You remember where I live," he asked.

"Short Branch?"

"Still there," he said. "Eat supper with me tomorrow night. I'll throw some dead cow on the grill and I'll listen to your thoughts." He looked up at me. "Anything else, Chief?"

"Nope."

"Then could we please get on with this moving detail. I've got things to do," he said.

"That's what worries me," I said.

"Be clear, old friend," he said. "You ain't my boss in this."

"You've never had a boss your whole life, W.B. But I am your friend," I said. "If that doesn't mean something, you need to tell me now."

He dropped the smoke and smashed it with his boot. "It does," he said. "Now, can we please go?"

CHAPTER 6

It was dusk when I got the dog and all the gear back to the cabin. When I dropped W.B. off at his vehicle he said nothing else about Tiller Mabry or cancer.

Berit acted like a puppy, running around the place, sniffing, and marking, and running back and forth from the porch to the woods, and then settled on a place by the front door to lay for awhile.

I stashed my gear and clothes and restocked the bar. I made one drink and moved to the front porch with the dog. She got up, moved across the porch with clicking nails on the wood and placed her head on my hand. After a while, I dialed my younger daughter's number in Rhode Island.

"Hi, Dad," she said.

"Hey, Abby. You okay?" I asked.

"Yeah, I'm driving home. Are you okay?" she asked.

"Yeah, just a change in schedule for awhile, and I thought I should tell you," I said.

"What's up?" she said.

"I resigned as Chief and took a wildlife officer job in a little county on Kentucky Lake," I said.

Long pause. "Okay," she said professionally. "And I guess you have a good reason for that move, so talk to me," she said.

"For the first time in a year, I'm challenged, and apprehensive," I said.

"Apprehensive?" she said. "That's a new idea for me, thinking you scared of anything."

"Yeah, me too," I said. "But I'm okay and the house is there for you and Clark to use when you come south. You still have a key, right?"

"Forget the key, Dad," she said. "Talk to me."

"I am," I said. "And the sound of your voice is good for me."

"Dad, I'll come right now, if you need me. I can catch a flight and be there in five hours," she said.

"I know you would," I said. "But I'm fine, Abby. If I can remember what happy is, I'm closer than I've been in a while, so I didn't call for you to worry. I called because I love you."

"Promise?" she asked.

"Promise," I said. "You've got my number."

"Call you every day," she said.

"Don't do that," I said. "Just call if you need me. You won't believe where I found a house. You have to see it," I said.

"Dad?"

"Yes."

"What's happy to you now?"

I thought about that. "I slept all night last night for the first time since your mom died," I said. "You're the shrink, tell me what that means."

"It could just mean you're really tired," she said. "It could mean you're finally restful with the idea of being alone. Or Dad, it could mean that she's watching and came back down and crawled in bed next to you," she said with a quivering voice.

"That's not very scientific," I said trying to say something to change her mood.

"Science cannot prove I love you, Dad," she said. "But I do."

"I love you, too, Abby. Say your prayers."

"Amen," she said. "Bye."

It was dark now and the crickets were drumming the temperature, cooler than last night, I was sure. I thought about making another drink, but hesitated and then thought better of it. It was a good thing...

My phone rang. It was W.B.

"Tell me the truth," he said. "You believe in God?"

I didn't stall for time. "Absolutely," I said.

"Why?"

"I never thought I'd have a religious conversation with you, W.B."

"Just answer the damn question," he demanded.

"Several times in my life, W.B. I had nothing left. I asked for strength. He gave me some," I said. "But understand, it did not come from me."

"Do you believe, if there is a God, that he could put people in your path for a reason?"

I thought about that for a second. "Not sure about that one, W.B., What do you think?"

"I think you coming here is proof that He does, or it's a damn fine coincidence," he said. "You been drinking?"

"One, "I said.

"I need you right now," he said.

"For what?"

"There's a friend of mine in the Humphreys County jail. He's eighteen and has nobody but me and his mom and she ain't around. I can't help him for several reasons, one being that I'm a bit drunk."

"How long's he been there?"

"Since three yesterday morning. I just got the call," he said.

"What'd he do?" I asked.

"He beat the shit out of some thugs who poached some deer on his property and kinda shot up their truck," he said. "I need you to interview him and the bad guys. They got taken in, too."

"I'll get right there," W.B. "Don't worry. I'll take care of it."

I heard W.B sigh. "Thanks," he said. "I owe you."

"No, you don't. What's his name?"

"John Russell," he said. "And Ethan, he's a damn fine young man. I'll explain later."

CHAPTER 7

It was nine o'clock before I pulled into the Humphreys County jail. I presented my I.D. to the front desk and asked to see John Russell.

"How come W.B. didn't come?" he asked.

"I'm fillin' in," I said.

"What about the other guys?" I asked.

"What?"

"The bad guys John Russel beat the shit out of," I said.

"What about them?" he asked.

"'Are they still here and what kinda shape are they in?"

"Yeah, I still got 'em. Moto's face ain't pretty," he said. "Cut up and black and blue and swollen. The Russell kid must be a fighter, cause Moto's whipped everybody around these parts. Takes pride in it."

The deputy led me down a hall and seated me in an interview room with one table and two chairs. He left the door open and returned in five minutes with a tall, well-built young man in handcuffs who wore a faded flannel shirt and jeans. Sandy brown hair and green eyes that looked right at you.

"Do me a favor and take the cuffs off," I asked.

The deputy did, and the kid sat across from me. "Who are you?" he asked.

"I'm Ethan Stewart," I said. "I'm the wildlife officer over in Houston County. W.B. sent me."

"I left W.B. a message. Didn't know if he got it or not," he said.

"So, how are you, John?"

"Well, I believe I'm in a bit of trouble or I wouldn't be here," he said.

"These other boys you fought are probably accusing you of some crimes, but don't worry about that right now. You just tell me what happened and then we'll see if I can't sort things out," I said.

"I'll tell you the truth, Mr. Stewart," he said.

"I know you will. Where's your mom?"

He paused and looked up. "She's with some relatives," he said.

"Can we contact her?" I asked.

"No sir. I mean I don't have a number."

"I see," I said. Well, first things first. Has the sheriff placed you under arrest?"

"No sir. Said he could hold us twenty-four hours to investigate what happened and after the game wardens interviewed us, he would make a decision."

"You need something to drink?" I asked.

"No sir. I'm okay. I'm just worried about having to stay here. My dogs need feeding," he said.

"Don't worry about your dogs, John. I promise W.B. or I will take care of them until you get out."

"I appreciate that," he said.

I paused. "You want to tell me what happened?"

"They shot a doe two nights ago on my farm. I heard the shot and ran through the woods where they were and tried to stop them, but they ran when I yelled at them. It was this guy named Moto's truck and he was there with another man. He was older, I think," he said.

"Why do you think, older?" I asked.

"The way he moved," he said. "I think it was his older brother, but I can't be sure."

"And then what happened?"

"The next day at school, I sent word to Moto to meet me on the football field after school. He came with three other boys, Carl and Topper and Tommy Askew. I told Moto I saw what he did and to never let me catch him or his truck on my property again. And when I told him that, he swung at me, so I hit him several times and then the Askew boy ran at me and I kneed him. He had his head down, trying to tackle me, I guess, and I remember not wanting to knee him in the head. I think I broke his collarbone. He piled up crying. And Moto was down, cussin' and screaming."

"How hard did you hit Moto?" I asked. "I heard his face isn't a pretty sight."

"As hard as I could. I guess that's pretty hard," John said. "But on Moto's best day, he's not real pretty," he said.

"I heard Moto's pretty tough," I said.

"He can't box," John said. "That's all I know."

"And you can?" I asked.

"Yes sir. I can.

"Who taught you how to box," I asked

"Box or fight?"

"There's a difference?" I asked.

He smiled. "Yes sir. The last place we lived, I had one of those big brothers. You know the Big Brother Program? Well, my big brother was a real good boxer. He taught me."

"What was his name?"

"Tyler Jones. He was in the Navy like my father. I sure wish he was here," he said.

"Your father alive?"

"No sir. He died when I was one. He was a Navy SEAL and died somewhere in Africa, I'm told. Tyler Jones was a SEAL, too. I think that's why he liked me, you know, them both being soldiers."

"It's a shame you never knew him…your Dad, I mean. I bet he was a fine man," I said.

"Yes sir, he was. But I know him. I've got this shoebox at home and it's full of letters he wrote me…addressed to me and everything. He wrote me every day he was there."

"Every day?"

"Yes sir. I have over a hundred letters."

"What would he talk about? In the letters, I mean?"

"Oh, he'd tell me about things over there…the people. He told me how he wished he could see me. He told me about how much he loved Mom and what a good woman she was. And he always ended with a wisdom of living. Lots of times it was the same words at the end… 'Never do or say anything without a good reason.' That was his motto," he said.

"That's some good advice," I said. "This Tyler Jones…did he ever talk war?"

"Sometimes, but not a lot. He would get this far away look in his eyes and he would tell me things. Must have been bad memories, 'cause sometimes he would get the wet eyes and then he would snap out of it and it was like he never mentioned it."

"Where was that, where you lived before here?"

"Little town in Arkansas, on the White River," he said.

"I see," I said. "And who taught you how to fight?"

John gave a quick smile and then withdrew it. "W.B. taught me the difference in boxing and fighting. He also introduced me to a friend of his who instructed me in fighting. Man, he was real good. And W.B. also taught me how to shoot. W.B. is the best shot I ever saw. No, W.B. is the best shot I ever heard of," he said.

"How did you meet W.B.?"

"When we first moved here, he came by and introduced himself. I was scared of him at first, but Mom said he was a good man and he is. He's been real good to me."

"He is a good man," I said.

"He must like you," he said.

"Why?"

"You're here. He sent you," he said. "W.B. lives by my father's motto."

I looked at him and couldn't say anything for a second.

"What happened after the fight?" I asked.

"I figured since Moto got whipped in front of his friends, he would try something else. So I slept outside. About two in the morning, I heard a truck pull in my driveway. I saw them get out and carry a dead deer to our porch. And then they threw a brick through the front window. I heard the glass break. And then they ran back to the truck, except they couldn't leave, cause I snuck down to the truck and took the keys."

"What did you do then?"

"I stepped out of the dark and asked where his truck was? He said 'right there.' And I said, 'And where are you?' And he said, 'Right here.' And I said, 'What did I tell you?' And he said, 'You said never to let me see you or your truck on my property.' So I started with the tires and then the glass and then the body. I shot the truck with my 870 until it didn't look like a truck anymore. And then I made them get the deer off the porch and bury it in my front yard with their hands."

"Did you ever point the gun at them?"

"If I did, they'd be dead. No sir, I didn't."

"Did you ever threaten to shoot them?"

"No sir. They pretty much did what I said after the truck got shot."

"Wouldn't it have been easier to call W.B.? Just report the deer being shot. He would have handled it legally," I said.

"But they were on my property," he said. "And I told them not to. My word has to mean something, don't you think?"

"Then with all respect, John. Be careful about what you say," I said. "Don't put yourself in conflict with the law."

"Am I in bad trouble?" he asked.

I smiled at him. "It is not a good thing to shoot up a vehicle, John. Yes, you are in some trouble, I suspect."

"Well, he used the truck to come to my house and throw a brick through my window. And I can tell you what would have happened if I hadn't been armed. I would have been hurt real bad if I had just gone outside and said 'Please don't do that.' So, I figured shootin' the truck stopped the violence between us. And it did. And I believe shootin' the truck was better than shooting them. Don't you? So, in the end, I made them understand that when I say something, I mean it. I think they'll remember the next time."

"I do think they'll remember. And I think you'll remember sitting in this room and the handcuffs and the jail cell," I said.

"I'm okay with what I did, Mr. Stewart," he said. "I hate my dogs are hungry, because of what those boys did to my property. If they had left me alone, none of this would have happened, right?"

"Point taken, John, but they did and you did and the law says what's right," I said.

"No sir. With all respect. The law says what's legal. Not all the time what's right," he said.

"I'll drink to that," I said. "But trust me, John, the law is what can put your butt in jail, and I want you to remember that. Avoid jail. Avoid felony charges. They can make your life very difficult."

The kid looked up from the table and straight at me. "Life is hard, Mr. Stewart. Sometimes, it's all I can do to hang on."

His words took me by surprise. And I looked away before saying, "Been there, son. Keep hangin' on. It'll ease up directly. You have my word." I stood up. "The sheriff will probably place you under arrest shortly. When he does, say nothing else to anyone. I'll get you a lawyer, if needed. You won't be in here long, I promise. And don't worry about the dogs."

John Russell stood up and shook my hand. It was a man's handshake. "I appreciate your help," he said.

CHAPTER 8

Moto was escorted into the interview room. I didn't ask that his cuffs be removed. He was enormous in size, with greasy, black hair and a scruffy beard. His left eye was still swollen shut and black. Right cross. His nose was cut, as well as his left cheek. Jabs. The kid could fight.

"Are you gonna arrest me?" he said.

"Nope, not yet," I said.

"Then I'll be leaving," he said rising from his chair.

"You've been watching too much T.V.," I said. "Sit your ass in that chair."

He reluctantly sat.

"Now," I said. "Tell me what happened yesterday."

"I don't remember," he said smiling.

"Who made your face ugly?" I asked.

"I fell."

"John Russell whipped your ass, didn't he?"

"He sucker punched me," he said looking away.

"No. Tell the truth. You swung first, didn't you?"

"I am tellin' the truth. Why would I lie about that? He sucker punched me when I wasn't lookin'. I can take his ass any day."

"Sure you can," I said. "You look like it. Now, who threw the brick through John Russell's window?"

"What brick?"

"What brick? Did you say, 'What brick?'" I looked at him across the table and his eyes left mine. "The SAME brick that came from the back of your truck. The SAME brick that has deer blood on it that will match the blood in the bed of your truck and the blood on John Russell's front porch, and the deer buried in John Russell's front yard. THAT brick."

Moto looked down at the table and fiddled with his cuffs. "I ain't sayin' nothin' else," he mumbled.

"Do you own the truck?" I asked.

"Yeah," he said.

"Is it paid for?" I asked.

"Yeah," he said. "Why?"

"Cause when I'm through with the charges against you, the state will own it," I said.

"Big damn deal," he said. "It's shot all to hell anyway."

I smiled. "It is a big deal," I said. "You're just too stupid to figure it out."

Moto looked up. "What?"

"You see, the only charge that could possibly be brought against John Russell is the destruction of your truck. Probably felony destruction of property. But it's hard for you to file charges against him, when the State owns the truck, don't you think?

"Huh?"

"Mr. Russell didn't shoot your truck. He shot my truck," I said. "And I don't care."

Moto looked defeated. "What's gonna happen to me?"

"That depends on how smart you are," I said. "I've got you on two counts of shooting big game out of season, illegal possession of deer in closed season, and a couple of more charges less serious, but the bottom line is that I'm gonna take your truck, the guns and equipment used in the violation, fine you several thousand dollars and take your hunting privileges for three years. I also will ask for jail time, which I'll get after the sheriff charges you with vandalism and reckless endangerment."

Moto exhaled. "What does smart mean?"

"It means no charges are filed against John Russell, and I don't ask for jail time," I said. "So, Mr. Moto, how smart are you?"

I greeted the ugly dog at the front door about midnight. She followed me through the house and then barked once for me to let her outside. I stood at the porch rail and watched her run through the yard and mark new ground before coming back to me. She looked up at me like she wanted me to say something, but I didn't.

I looked at the sky. Brilliant stars in a clear black eternity. Eternity. Thoughts of forever still made my head swim and I thought of a line in *Out of Africa*... 'God is laughing at us.' Maybe He is. Half way through my interview with John Russell, I had realized I was interviewing myself.

I rested on the porch rail and wondered if Taylor James was still awake. I also wondered if she wondered if I was awake. If not sleeping, I wondered where she was. I flipped open my phone and scrolled the contacts to her saved number. I stared at the number with my thumb on the call button, paused, and hung up. I would call her tomorrow.

The phone vibrated in my hand and I jumped. I checked the number.

"You must be psychic?" I asked.

"No," she said. "Just careful. Why?"

"Nothing," I said.

"Are you home?" she asked.

"Just," I said.

"Okay," she said. "Just checking. Goodnight."

"Wait," I said quickly.

"Yes," she said finally.

"Why did you ask if I'm home?"

She paused. "I guess I should have told you, but I forgot. I have a security camera with an alarm. I can't see your driveway from my house and I had problems with vandals. I saw a vehicle lights on the camera."

"I see. So you were asleep?"

Long pause. "No," she said.

"Why not? It's late," I said.

"You're not asleep," she said.

"I've been working," I said.

"I've been reading," she said.

"What are you reading?"

"A book," she said. "It's very deep."

"Where are you? Right now."

"Where are you?" she asked back.

"Sitting on the porch steps looking at the stars," I said. "You ever do that?"

"Not in a long time," she said.

"Why?" I asked.

"I'm not sure," she said. "I just quit looking I guess."

"Don't," I said. "Quit looking."

She didn't say anything for a few seconds. "Explain that." she said.

"I think that sometimes I get so caught up in…stuff….I lose track of little things, like pondering the stars," I said. "And you never answered my question."

"I'm in my bedroom," she said. "And I can't seem to lead you away from uncomfortable questions."

"I'm unleadable," I said. "A fault of my character, I guess."

"Anything else?"

"Would you read me the last paragraph you read?" I said.

"Why?"

"Cause I'm suddenly interested in what kind of book you would read."

"It's really late," she said.

"Are you being honest?" I asked.

"Accurate, but not honest," she said. She paused. "I may not want to read to you, that's all."

"Why?"

"Because you may judge me by the book I choose to read."

"I will," I said. "And that's fair, I think."

"Only if you pick something to read to me is it fair," she said.

"Tonight?" I asked. "It's really late."

She laughed and I could see in my memory her smile and her laugh lifted me somehow. And then she was reading, without warning, and her voice was different somehow, like she was telling a story important for me to hear. I hung on every word, every inflection of her voice, and lay back on the cool porch watching the stars.

"'In the afternoon, after the storm had passed heading east into the mountains, she watched him sleep on the couch in his den. She had driven him home from the doctor's office, after eighteen stitches, and the pig's feet and Fatboy hugging her goodbye and Billy Browder apologizing to her on the front steps of the store. It seemed all out of sinc to her, the memories hop-scotching in front of each other until there was nothing left but her vision of him asleep on the couch. She watched him for a long time, lost in the feeling of just being there, at this particular moment in time, with this man, in this house, in this country, with these people. After a while she retrieved her journal from the pack and wrote:'"

"Don't stop," I said.

"That's the last paragraph. That's what you asked," she said.

"What did she write in the journal?"

"Read the book and find out," she said.

"Do you loan books?" I asked.

"Sometimes. Depends on the person asking," she said.

"I'm asking," I said.

There was a long silence. "Who are you?" she asked. "Really. I want to know. Every word out of your mouth warns my brain you are one very shrewd man, and every word out of your mouth tells my heart you are just the most honest person I've ever met. I'm not one to delay important questions, so there it is…the question I've wanted to ask you since last night. Which is it?"

I shut my eyes. "I'm honest to a fault with certain people…completely vulnerable. But not many," I whispered.

"Me?" she asked.

"You," I said. "And don't ask me to explain it because I can't."

"Then I'll loan you the book," she said. "Goodnight, Ethan Stewart."

"Don't," I said.

"Don't what?"

"Don't hang up," I said. "You don't have to talk. Just don't hang up."

"Are you okay?" she asked.

"Shhhh…just don't hang up."

She paused for a long time. "Goodnight, Ethan." And hung up.

CHAPTER 9

W.B. woke me up at five a.m. "How'd you do that?" he asked over the phone.

"What?" I asked.

"I just picked John up and took him home," he said. "No charges were filed."

"I just gave Mr. Moto a chance to do the right thing," I said.

"Thanks," he said. "See you this afternoon."

At first light the sky was cloudy, with a fog that lay in the hollows. After coffee, Berit and I walked the path to Taylor's house. Dew dripped from the trees like rain. After four hundred yards on the forested path, it led to a horseshoe bottom with her house visible on a hill overlooking the creek. It was of southwestern design and too large for one person, and then I remembered it was originally the home of her parents. There were horses in the pasture and a large barn stood behind the house. I saw her washing Jasper in a watering trough from across the field.

I thought about stepping from the trees and walking to her, but turned and walked the path back to the cabin. From my experience, one should never interrupt a woman washing a dog, particularly this hour of the day. The dog is generally in trouble for rolling in something stinky, which makes the woman less than social.

An hour later, I was driving to Erin to check on the status of Spike Mabry. The radio sounded.

"Thirteen hundred to thirteen twenty-one."

I paused. Is that my new number? I grabbed a radio book and looked me up while I drove. "Yep." I was hoping this could be delayed a few days...

I grabbed the microphone. "Thirteen twenty-one."

"Ten twenty?"

"Tennessee Ridge headed to Erin," I said.

"Meet me at the courthouse," he said flatly.

"When?" I asked for fun.

"Now," he said.

I didn't respond.

"Thirteen-twenty-one?"

"Thirteen-twenty one."

"You get that last transmission?" he barked.

"Yes," I said. "You said, 'Thirteen twenty-one'."

"No," he said. "Meet me at the courthouse now."

"Can't be there, now," I said. "It'll take about ten minutes."

He never responded and I could imagine him throwing the mike. We have disliked each other since he was hired and I have never hidden my disrespectful feelings for him. Not very professional, I admit, but he deserves it all, and more.

When I parked at the courthouse, he was waiting in his vehicle. I tapped on his window and he looked up. He glanced at me and then back at the document he was pretending to read.

I turned and walked away. He saw me leaving and immediately followed. "Where do you think you're going?" he said.

"To the jail," I said. "You looked busy."

"You could wait," he said. "I need to talk to you."

"I could wait for you, Benny, but I won't," I said. We were now face to face under a red oak in the courthouse side yard.

"Look," he said. "You're mine now. I'm not sure why you were demoted, but you work for me, now. And you are out of uniform."

"Actually, Benny, I'm not. Administrative Directive Number 12 states that when an officer is not in uniform, he must display the badge and be armed with a weapon he has qualified with during training. As you can see, my badge is displayed and I am carrying a legal weapon."

"I require my officers to always be in issued uniforms when driving that state vehicle," he said.

"But of course, you realize, Benny, that you have neither scheduled an interview with me to explain your procedures, nor have you sent me anything in writing, so until the time you officially do those things, Benny, I am acting under the policy of the Agency."

"I really think you enjoy this," he said. "You won't for long."

"I don't enjoy talking to you at all. I always hate talking to idiots, but sometimes in this job, we are forced to," I said.

His upper lip quivered as he looked at me. "Be careful. You ain't Chief no more," he said.

"You be careful, Benny," I said. "And don't you ever forget that I'm not now nor will I ever be 'yours.'" And I turned and walked to my truck. So much for a brotherly working relationship with my supervisor.

CHAPTER 10

W.B. built his house on a hill overlooking a long valley. He bought enough land to buffer the valley from distant neighbors who might complain about the sound of gunfire, but most folks in this country didn't seem to mind the sound. He built the house as logistic support for the game warden job and his shooting. Nothing more.

I found him behind the house at the shooting bench. Below, in the valley, were berms at hundred yard increments out to a thousand yards. Wind flags flew at each target stand. The distance of his targets was mind boggling. He looked up briefly as I left the Jeep, but then went back to the scoped rifle on the bags.

"Watch your ears," he said.

I plugged my ears with my fingers and the rifle roared. In the far distance I heard the bullet hit steel and watched as the six hundred yard gong swung violently backwards and then righted itself. He looked up and smiled. Well, it was a W.B. smile…not a real one.

"I'm gonna leave this rifle to you, Ethan," he said. "It has served me well."

"3-0-8?" I asked.

"Yep."

"You don't look sick to me," I said.

"Looks can be deceiving," he said.

"Is it time to have a drink?" I asked.

"Almost," he said. "Spot me first. Sit down there and get in that spotting scope on the table and watch the target at four hundred yards. Fresh target. Two inch orange bull," he said. He rested the .308 in a gun rack and lifted another rifle to the bench. It was green, synthetic stocked and military in its appearance, with a big bull barrel, and a tactical NIGHTFORCE scope.

"What caliber?" I asked.

"260 Remington," he said. "The most aerodynamic bullet I've ever shot. Great B.C. Low recoil. Less wind drift than the 308. Extremely accurate. German barrel, handmade stock."

"What range?" I asked.

"Good out to eight hundred, maybe a tad farther on a good day with the velocity I'm loading," he said. "All I need out of it now is extreme reliability in accuracy to four hundred."

"Why four hundred?"

He didn't answer. "Watch the bull," he said.

I settled in behind the spotting scope and adjusted the focus. The target crystallized at thirty power…perfectly clear. "Send it," I said, and I heard the gun report. I watched the bullet arc and push a wavy cone of air toward the target. And then there was a black hole in the bull.

"Twelve o clock at the top of the orange," I reported.

The next two shots were fast, particularly for a bolt gun. Two holes appeared in the center of the orange, maybe an inch apart. "Damn, W.B.," I whispered.

He looked up, collected his brass, and placed them in a plastic shell box. "They in the bull?"

"Yes sir," I said. "Three shot group, maybe one inch. That's quarter minute accuracy."

"The gun's a shooter. We'll see if it's a faithful partner," he said. "Sometimes, they're fickled."

Later, with the coals glowing and one brown whisky nursed, he threw the meat on the grill. He refilled my glass and we sat in the yard in old wooden chairs watching the sun fade.

"You have a nice place here, W.B.," I said.

"It'll do," he said. "But it ain't New Mexico."

"New Mexico?"

"Went there once hunting mule deer. Northern mountains. Prettiest place I ever took a breath."

"Tell me about Tiller Mabry," I said. "I need background."

"He's a mad dog," he said. "Very aggressive and very smart. The badge doesn't intimidate him. Actually, it attracts him. He loves confrontation. There was word a few months back that he confronted a business man out of Nashville at the boat ramp one day, leaving the man on the ground crying without a punch ever being thrown. The Mabry brothers laughed at the man, as he cowered while his family watched, under the power of backwoods intimidation. It seems the words from a whiskered chin, said with all sincerity, that ended with, 'I'll cut yore fuckin' head clean off and throw it to yore little girl,' was more than the banker from Brentwood could stand."

I nodded. "Where'd he come from? Any family stuff I need to know?"

"Everybody knows his past around here. His mother, Lola, married Oscar Mabry and had three sons. When Tiller was eleven, his father was killed by a cousin, Lyle Tanner, at Three Springs one hot July night. Lyle, a seriously purposeful man, killed Oscar with a hawk-billed knife over a gun trade. Lyle then married Lola, who was present at the killing, to keep her from testifying against him. The grand jury returned a No True Bill, and Lyle went free, moved into the Mabry house and raised the three boys as his own. Tiller grew up in conflict with his step-father and the law, gaining a reputation of instant retaliation against anybody who crossed him. He dealt in guns and whiskey and drugs and stolen property, but his passion was poaching. We've convicted Tiller three times for killing deer out of season, and the judge took his hunting privileges for life. Seems the locals will turn him loose for violent crimes, but bust his ass for poaching. It's a cultural thing, you see."

I nodded. "I heard he was into mussel buying and selling," I said.

"He got into the mussel industry at the peak of the Japanese buying spree. And the money got real serious. Lately, he's been into Kentucky Lake caviar with the Russians. And our young friend, Samuel," and he stopped. "What a damn fine kid he was." W.B. looked at me. "Samuel was going to bring the whole thing down by sending Tiller to jail for murder."

"Anything else?" I asked.

"I've said enough for now. I'm waiting on you," he said.

"Okay, I'll tell you what I know. You add or correct if I'm weak," I said.

He took a sip and started a fresh cigarette.

"It started with the search warrant for an illegal deer at the Mabry house. Samuel had a C.I. that gave credible information about two deer transported in the back of a red, Olds Cutlass, that ended up in the Mabry home freezer. Samuel got the search warrant and with a deputy went to the house. A man named Stump Poodle was sitting behind an open screened door. Samuel opened the door to speak and they heard crashing in the back. They entered the house, told Stump to stay put, left the warrant with him, and proceeded to the kitchen where the Mabry brothers were flushing dope down the drain. All the bad guys were high. Tiller tried to cut Samuel with a kitchen knife and Samuel busted his arm with the MAG-LIGHT. The others gave up real quick with their big brother lying on the floor screaming. How am I doing so far?"

W.B. flicked an ash and nodded. "Go on," he said.

"The Olds was registered to Tiller Mabry and it was out back and that's where Samuel found the blood and hair in the trunk. Only after analysis, it wasn't just deer blood. Human blood was also found, belonging to one missing mussel diver named Oslo Janks. And after some thoughtful interrogation of youngest brother Edward Mabry by the T.B.I., he turned on his brothers and gave up the location of Mr. Janks, who they found buried in an old grave with a tombstone of some guy who died in 1869 or something. And then the state is ready to go to court, with Samuel as the primary witness, when Samuel is killed on a stakeout at night. Two shots. One to the stomach as he stood by his door and the next to the head."

"Night shots with a .22 centerfire," W.B. said with a low voice. "Hardball ammo. .223. Two possibilities. Night vision scope or a really good scope with ample moonlight at close range. I checked the moon phase and there was hardly any moonlight that night. Had to be night vision scope...very expensive."

"Bottom line is that the jury convicted Tiller on the Jank's murder without Samuel's testimony," I continued. "But after the addition of a high dollar lawyer, who filed a post-conviction relief petition, the judge reversed the conviction based on the fact that Samuel never announced the warrant before entering the house, which suppressed all the evidence collected by the search. The second trial, without the evidence, went for Tiller."

"And on the way out of the court room, Tiller turned to us and laughed," W.B. said. "That was three weeks ago. He just walked away."

"And my question to you, old friend, is how do we know that Tiller Mabry killed our friend? Where's the proof that he's guilty? How do we know for sure?" I asked.

W.B. got up and turned the meat. He never looked at me while he spoke and I strained to hear every word. "Tiller Mabry didn't kill our friend," he said. "But he had him killed. He hired a hood out of Chicago. A cousin of theirs that grew up here and left twenty years ago. Been in and out of prison ten times. They called him Slack. Paid him five hundred dollars to kill Samuel."

"How do you know?" I asked.

W.B. sat back down and took a drink. "Well, we forgot early on that we ain't the only ones upset about

Tiller walking," he said. "The family of Oslo Janks, backwoods as they are, were pissed. They did an investigation of their own, backwoods style, which involved a bunch of whiskey and maybe some arm twisting. Remember, they all run in the same bunch."

"Where's Slack now?" I asked.

"Dead," he said. "Under thirty feet of water in Kentucky Lake. I have a GPS coordinate when we need it," he said.

"And you have this knowledge on good information?" I asked.

"Yeah, and I ain't about to give up my informant, no offense. You know how it goes. But he's never lied to me before," W.B. said.

"I guess that means you don't think he's lying now," I said.

"I've tested him forty different ways," W.B. said. "Little things, like when he was with them, who was there, who said what. It all plays out. You see, Tiller convinced the Janks boys that Slack killed Oslo. Of course, Slack wasn't even in Tennessee when Oslo was killed, but what the hell, they were all drunk and it made sense at the time. And Tiller got all this done from jail, don't forget. There is a string of conversations here. I mean, Tiller's one weakness is that he had to tell people things to get this murder done and my C.I. is in the middle of it. In fact, my guy was paid to dump Slack's body."

"How long you been sitting on this?" I asked.

"Not long," he said. "It all started when Tiller walked. And then there was the minor problem of me findin' out I'm dyin' and all, which upset my normal thinkin' for a spell."

"I still don't see proof that Tiller had Samuel killed," I said. "All you've got is testimony, if you're lucky, from a bunch of guys that aren't real up-standing citizens."

"True," W.B. said. "And don't forget, Tiller planned the whole thing. He wanted Slack dead, the only person who could testify that Tiller hired him to kill Samuel. He wanted the Janks boys satisfied they had the killer of Oslo. And one more thing." He leaned forward as he spoke. "I think Tiller wanted me to know he planned it all."

"Why?," I asked.

"Because he's that arrogant," W.B. said. "He's sending us a message. I'm convinced the son of a bitch told my C.I. to give him up. He wants me to know he didn't actually pull the trigger. He wants me to know we don't have a case against him. He wants me to know the truth, because the truth among backwoods boys is not damaging to normal folks on a jury. You see, Chief, our legal system works among honorable people, with honest folks testifying, but it fails when all the witnesses can lie with precision."

I didn't say anything because he was right. But it didn't matter because I had a plan to surround it. I had a plan that cut to the heart of it. I waited and then looked across the darkness toward my friend. "This is much deeper than justice," I said. "This is about our ability to legally deal with bad people who beat the system. And, deal with our own demons, namely vengeance. And vengeance can corrupt us if we don't handle this right."

"Go on," he said.

"I want to confront Tiller Mabry with the truth…legally. I want to give the man a last chance to do right and admit his guilt. I want to bring the truth to him and make him suffer with it."

"How much did you drink before you got here?" he said. "He doesn't give one rat's ass about the truth."

"I want to confront Tiller, myself," I said. "I want to tell him that we know everything and ask him to admit his guilt. I want him to think I am that desperate to plead to his sense of goodness. I want to see if his demons can be beaten. We pick a place where he feels totally safe and thinks I'm completely alone. I'll show him I'm not armed. I want to be totally vulnerable and simply ask him to do the right thing. I want to offer him a last chance to find some honor."

"And he may kill you, too," he said. "You are aware of that?"

I paused. "Yep. He may try, particularly if he thinks he can get away with it. That's why we record the whole thing. Video and audio. I still have my spook contacts and they will help me."

"So you will have it documented that they killed your ass," he said. "That's real honorable."

"Not if you're as good as I think you are," I said.

W.B. smiled through the darkness. "I see," he said.

"You are my back-up," I said. "From far, far away."

"It's still dangerous," he said. "I mean, the son of a bitch will die, if he shoots you. I promise you that, but the timing is really close."

"What do you think he'll do?" I asked.

"Depends on his mood, I'd say. Whether he's drunk or hung over or high. Whether he's had a bad day. He's a temperamental sort. Can't stand a man acting superior. That's where you'll get him mad," he said.

"I'm not trying to piss him off, W.B.," I said.

"Uh huh."

"I'm serious," I said. "That's not my intention."

"And I'm not intending to kill him," he said.

"Give me your word," I said.

"What?"

"You will not kill him, unless it's to protect me from getting killed."

W.B. pondered those words for a while. "I said earlier that I owe you. I do," he said. "You have my word."

"Just so we're clear," I said.

"We're clear. But don't forget that I've stood by your side in touchy situations over the years. I know you, Ethan Stewart. I've watched you work, and you could make the Pope swing at you, if you wanted, and never raise your voice."

"That's not what I'm doing, W.B."

"Okay, but they'll think we set him up," he said. "I mean, if he dies."

"We will probably end up in court," I said. "But we'll win. I will only ask him to do the right thing. Talking is legal. You only back me up because he has a record of violence."

"What if he doesn't play…either way? No admission and no threats," he asked.

"Then we do it again," I said. "Over and over. I'm not going away."

W.B. got up and moved the sizzling meat from the grill to a platter and turned to me. "I got no problem with offerin' a feller a last chance, before I kill him," he said. "Let's eat." And he walked away toward the house.

I sat there for a while and studied on things. The world, as we know it, is relative. As a kid I always wondered if the red apple I was eating looked the same to my friends. They knew what they were seeing was a red apple, but was red the same for all of us? It was possible, I figured, they could see blue and knew it as red. I wondered about the world through Tiller Mabry's eyes.

Supper was quiet in the house and we never spoke of it again, until he asked me, "When is all this going down? Don't have just a heap of time, ya know."

"Give me a few days," I said. "I need to do some things first."

He nodded.

"So, tell me about the kid, John Russell," I said.

CHAPTER 11

I stopped at the entrance to the cabin and looked at my watch. Nine. I dialed her number. It rang four times.

"Hello."

"Is your security camera still on?"

"Do you want it on?"

"I just wanted to report I'm home, so you'd know it's me."

"Thanks," she said. "Long day?"

"They're all long," I said. "I owe you four hundred dollars. I haven't forgotten."

"Neither have I," she said. "Want a drink?"

I smiled. "Yes, ma'am. I do. Your place or mine?"

"They're both still my places," she said.

"Okay, where you sleep or where I sleep?"

"I don't sleep," she said.

"That would be a medical miracle," I said.

"Come to the big house, where you saw me washing the dog this morning," she said.

"I suddenly don't feel very game wardenish," I said. "I must be losing my covert skills."

"The horses. I saw the horses see you. Can't fool a horse," she said.

"I'll be right there," I said. "Do you have a dress code?"

"Yes, I do," she said. "You must be dressed."

I closed the phone and it rang immediately.

"Hello."

"Dad, where are you? I've been by the house and Ugly Dog is gone and you're gone and no note or anything."

"Hey, Lizzy. I'm gonna be out of town for a while."

"How long?"

"Maybe a year."

"A year! Dad! What's going on?"

"I changed jobs. You need money?"

"No. Well, I could use some, but forget that. Why would you leave without telling me?"

"Not exactly sure where you were, Liz."

"I have a phone, Dad?"

"With minutes?"

"Yeah. I got minutes."

"Well, you found me and you can always call me. I'm fine, Liz. Keep an eye on the house for me, but you can't live there."

"Okay, Daddy. I love you."

"I love you too. Always have. Always will. You have Abby's number?"

"Yes sir."

"Good. Take care, Lizzy."

"Bye, Daddy."

I pulled down her long driveway and I walked to the front door, a massive thing with ornamental iron décor. I rang the bell and I heard her yell from the side of the house.

"Walk around back!"

I found her on a veranda, of sorts, looking over the pasture that stretched in the darkness to the creek. Crickets sounded at the wood line, and a barred owl called in the distance. Jasper looked up at me as I approached and then lay his head back down. There was a bottle of brown whiskey, a bucket of ice and two glasses at the table where she waited. Candle lanterns flickered casting a yellow light across her, and she watched me as I approached. Her hair was pulled back into a thick pony tail. She wore a long-sleeved, blue denim shirt, rolled up to her elbows and faded jeans. She was barefoot and when I was close enough to see, her feet were tanned. She smiled up at me.

"Have a seat," she said. "Rest."

"You're barefooted," I said while sitting.

She just looked at me.

"I mean, I noticed your feet are tan."

She put ice in our glasses with her hand and poured her drink.

And I did the same.

"Barefooted feels good. You should try it," she said.

I looked at my boots. "Not sure that's a good idea."

"Bashful?" she asked.

"My feet may stink," I said without thinking.

"I'm upwind, and if it's too bad, there's a hose on the side of the house. Now, take your boots off."

I poured a drink and tasted it. "My feet are not tanned like yours," I said. "And I cannot believe that matters," and I looked under the table at her tanned feet and then looked back at her. "But right now, at this particular place in time, it does."

She almost laughed, but held it, the smile broadening across her face. "How old are you?"

"How old do I look?" I asked.

"Fifty," she said. "It's the wrinkles around the eyes, but your eyes are very young," she said.

I gave her my best confident grin. "There is absolutely nothing wrong with my eyes," I said. "How old are you?" I asked quickly.

"How close was I?" she asked.

"Close enough," I said.

"Take your damn boots off, Ethan. I never figured a game warden to have Bahamas-tanned feet. You cannot relax on a warm evening with shoes on."

I placed the drink on the table and commenced to untying my Browning boots, pulled them off with a bit of a struggle and tossed them to the side. "There," I said. "Happy?"

She motioned with her glass. "Socks, too," she said.

And I did, throwing them in a pile by the boots. The cool air immediately relaxed me and I wiggled my toes in front of me. "Very nice," I said, taking another drink of whiskey.

"How old?" I asked again.

"Guess," she said.

"Not on your life," I said. "But if forced, not a day over thirty-nine."

She raised her glass and we touched the glasses together. "Close enough," she said. "Forty-three. How was your day?"

I thought of all the serious conversations of the day. "Just learning new country," I said. "But I did hear the most incredible story I've ever heard today."

She leaned on her elbows. "Tell me," she said. "I love good stories."

"Can I trust you to keep a confidence?" I asked. "He didn't tell me to keep it secret, but knowing the man, I suspect everything he says is confidential."

"Yes," she said. "But if I couldn't be trusted, I'd still say yes, so I guess you have to trust your instinct."

"If I didn't trust you, I'd never have taken by boots off," I said. "I'm very particular about who sees my feet," I said.

"Me, too," she said.

"Last night I went to the Humphreys County jail to interview a young man who is a friend of a friend. He was being held for shooting up a poacher's truck. Seems the bad guys threw a brick through the front window of his house and left a dead doe on his front porch, except the kid wasn't asleep and was waiting for them. With a shotgun."

"Did he shoot them?" she asked.

"No, just the truck and then made them bury the deer with their bare hands in his front yard," I said.

"Where were his parents? How old is he?"

"John Russell is eighteen. Good looking kid and good sized, too." I paused. "His father died when he was an infant. A Navy Seal operating in some clandestine mission in Africa. And young John Russell carries his father in a shoe box. Letters from a father in a war zone to his infant son about how to live and what is important all filed neatly away in a shoe box. And he's read them over and over through the years, so much that many of them are memorized and he repeats some of the wisdoms of his father like some badge of honor."

She wasn't smiling anymore and her eyes stayed on me as I talked. I turned to face her across the table.

"Ever heard anything like that?" I asked.

"No," she said. "Did he repeat any of the things his father told him?"

"Yes. 'Never do or say anything without a good reason,' is one that stuck in my memory."

She didn't say anything.

"My friend, name of W.B. Langford, was one of four soldiers who fought side by side with John's father. And W.B. was holding John's father as he died, and the father's last words were 'Promise me, see my boy knows how to be a good man.' And he made them promise. And he also made them promise to never tell John who they were…the relationship to him."

"Why?" she asked. "What difference…."

"He said it wouldn't be as strong that way. He wanted the boy to have the relationships as if they were completely his own," I said.

"What about the mother?" she asked.

And I had to pause. "She never remarried. In the early years she lived close to one of the soldiers. Then moved close to another team member. And for the last five years, she's been in Tennessee, living close to W.B. He's a wildlife officer."

"Where?" she asked.

"Humphreys County. And each soldier taught John Russell things they thought would be important to the father."

"Was she romantic with any of them?"

"I wondered the same," I said. "No. She never was attached to anyone after he died. And according to my friend, her heart was broken and never healed. She was kind, compassionate, and devoted to John Russell. And, I'm not sure she isn't the main influence on his life, even though he's one tough kid. He has gentleness about him, combined with the tough part."

"You said, 'was'," she said.

"She was very sick," I said "She wanted no funeral, just her son to lay her in the ground." And then my voice broke without warning, and I tried to clear my throat, but it burned and I finished it anyway with a trembling voice. "And so she died last month, alone with the son of her husband, and that young man carried his mother to the backyard, dug a grave, read scripture, buried her, and planted her favorite flowers as her tombstone."

And I looked away from her because I hadn't cried in a long time, not even at Jenny's funeral, although I wished I could, but now the tears were unstoppable in this yard of a stranger in a strange new place.

And I felt her hand take mine. Nothing else. No words. Just her fingers around my hand as I looked away and her touch was all I needed, like some refuge of understanding that made me even more grateful for her presence. And finally I turned to her and I could see her tears, but she smiled anyway.

"Ain't I something," I said. "Bare white feet and teary. Ruins any thoughts you had of me being a tough guy," I added.

"You can't even imagine my thoughts of you," she whispered.

"I hope that's a good thing," I said.

"It is," she said. "A good thing."

"Well," I said, changing the subject. "The problem now, the only family John Russell has is W.B.. No one else. And my friend was diagnosed with lung cancer last week."

"Does John know that?"

"No. And, John is afraid to tell anyone that his mom died because he's still in high school and until he's graduated he's afraid he'll lose the farm."

"Isn't that against the law? Not reporting a death?"

"Yes," I said. "W.B. took care of it. One of his best friends is the local doctor."

"Can I help?" she asked. "Does he need a job? A place to stay? Anything?"

"I'll check. Thanks," I said. "Oh yeah, almost forgot." I pulled a check from my shirt pocket and handed it to her. "I've got to go."

"Don't forget your boots," she said.

I picked them up. "Think I'll walk barefooted," I said. "Feels really good."

She smiled up at me. "You okay?" she asked.

"I'm fine," I said. "Thanks for...I keep thanking you when I leave."

"For what?"

"Thought about that a lot," I said. "Not quite sure yet. The thought of meeting someone here, like you, never crossed my mind."

"Mine either," she said. "You just never know, huh?"

"No, you don't," I said. "And you know something else? I've known W.B. Langford for almost fifteen years and never knew he was a SEAL. Things make more sense about him now."

"Like you said," she said. "You just never know."

"That's the fun part, Taylor. Getting pleasantly surprised. You try to sleep tonight," I said smiling.

"Think I'll sit out here for a while," she said. "And by the way, your feet don't stink."

"Like you said, you were upwind."

CHAPTER 12

The next morning I stopped by the courthouse to check on Spike Mabry's warrant and file a court date. I also wanted to know if Spike had filed a warrant against Julia. I climbed the steps to the second floor and entered the clerk's office. The clerk looked up at me as I entered, looked away, and then back at me quickly. She was about forty, dyed black hair, and her blouse was too tight, exposing way too perky breasts for her age.

"Good morning," she said smiling.

"Good morning to you," I said. "You must be Jackie."

"How'd you know?" she asked.

I pointed to the name plate on the desk in front of her. "I'm trained to be observant," I said.

"Oh," she said laughing. "Are you the new man?"

"I don't feel new," I said. "I just stopped by to check on a court date for Spike Mabry, who I arrested two days ago."

She thumbed through a stack of warrants and pulled one out. "Yeah, right here. Court set for next month. Always the first Tuesday. Starts at nine."

"Thanks," I said. "Did he file any warrants against anyone?"

"No," she said. "The Mabrys don't use our legal system to get back at people. And you should be very careful, Mr. Uh…"

"I'm Ethan Stewart," I said. "Pleased to meet you, Jackie."

"You're him, then," she said looking up at me bashfully.

"I'm sorry," I said.

"Your supervisor came by here yesterday and warned us about you," she said. "He said you had been demoted and might cause us some problems you being depressed and all."

I smiled at her. "Did he now," I said. "What else did he say?"

She looked around and we were the only people in the room. "Well, he did say you were having some alcohol problems."

"Let me ask you a question, Jackie. Just between you and me."

"Okay," she said.

"Do you like Officer Benny Alexander?"

"Why, no," she said. "He's really weird and gives me the creeps."

"Can you keep a secret?" I asked.

She zipped her lips with her finger and smiled. "Absolutely."

I paused. "No, I can't," I said. "I don't even know you."

"Look, Hon," she said. "Benny don't live in this county. You do, and I'm real faithful to my local officers."

"Promise?"

"I promise," she said.

I lowered my voice. "It won't matter if you report to Benny that you smelled whiskey on my breath. It fits my cover. It may help."

She looked confused. "I don't get it," she said.

I looked around to make sure no one was listening. "I'm with Internal Investigations. I'm here to watch Benny Alexander. Being depressed and drinking is my cover."

"For real," she said. "What did he do?"

I shook my head. "I better not say."

"You can't stop now, Honey. Don't tease me," she said.

I whispered. "He's using state vehicles to…uh…meet people in very backwoods places."

"An affair? Tell me. I may know her," she said with much excitement.

I winked. "It ain't a 'her', Jackie," I whispered.

She covered her mouth. "You don't mean it! He's gay?"

"Shhhh!" I said. "Look. I'm just down here to do a job. If you hear anything, let me know."

"I will, Baby. Mum's the word," she said, as I turned and left the room.

As I descended the courthouse steps, I saw him writing my license number on a newspaper, standing there like some meter reader with a job to do. He was medium sized and sinewy, and when he saw me approaching, he stepped back onto the sidewalk, lit a thin cigar, and rested his back against my truck. He stared at me. His eyes were dark and old acne scars pitted his cheeks. Dark complexioned.

"So you're the new carp cop," he said. "Been wanting to see you in person, tell you how sorry I am the last one got gut shot and all."

I stopped a safe distance from him and turned sideways. "Smoking those things will kill you," I said. "You should consider changing your life style."

He smiled, stepped to the sidewalk and moved toward me. *Stay calm.*

"You know who I am?" he asked.

"Yeah," I said. "Every hick town has one of you in it. Some reject from *Deliverance* who thinks he's bad. Thinking 'bad' will make him happy."

"You don't have a fucking clue what I think, Possum Sheriff," he said "If you did, you'd leave town tonight."

I looked hard at him and gave a little smile. "You gonna actually do something or just stand there looking pathetic."

He stepped closer. "I just wanted to say 'hi,'" he said. "Be neighborly and ask you to give Miss Julia a message. Tell her that Spike wants to see her again, you know, grab a bite and catch a movie."

"Yeah," I said. "I didn't know any cartoons were playing. You know, something a first grader could understand?"

He dropped the cigar and looked back at me. "Well, maybe I could get Taylor James to go with me and we could double date. Then me and Taylor could teach them a thing or two. You know, by watching us."

"Maybe you could," I said. "She might be needing some charity work. You know, for the underprivileged and illiterate. If you changed your life though, like go to church and help folks in need, confess your sins, you might have a shot."

"You weren't so Christian pure when you whipped Spike's ass the other day," he said. "Why the change in spirit?"

"Bad men with guns tend to modify my Christian gentleness," I added. "And Jesus would have slapped your brother too, I do believe."

He laughed out loud and backed away. "Are you for real?" he yelled mockingly.

"I'm real as death itself, but I'll pray for you, Tiller. My momma always said it's hard to hate a man you pray for."

His lip quivered for the first time. "Yore momma can kiss my country ass," he said. And then he smiled. "I'll take 'em young or old. It's all the same to me." And he waved to me as he backed away, crossed the street and left in a black Chevy truck, beating his fists against the steering wheel like a mad man.

CHAPTER 13

Over the next four hours, I visited three country stores, which also served as big game checking stations, and shook some hard-callused hands. I was invited to three home-cooked meals, two fishing trips, and offered hunting rights on several beautiful farms. I wish I had the time or the inclination to relax. I had neither.

I called Taylor and asked her to find Julia and meet me at my house in late afternoon. She asked why and I said I needed the follow up interview regarding the Spike incident. No need to scare them about Tiller's threats....yet.

On the way home that afternoon, I passed a dented Chevy truck parked on the side of the road, with an old man sitting on the tailgate petting a Feist dog. There was a double-barreled Stevens laying broken open beside him and four dead squirrels. I stopped and walked back to the truck.

"Howdy," I said. "Looks like you've made supper tonight."

He looked up. Steel blue eyes and white hair. The Feist wagged her docked tail and scooted sideways towards me. I briefly rubbed her head and then extended my hand to the old man.

"Name's Ethan Stewart," I said. "I'd ask to see your hunting license but I doubt you'd be sitting on the side of the road in plain sight, if you were hiding something."

"Don't hide much these days," he said. "Tend to outgrow that practice, if you live long enough," he said. "How 'bout you, you hide stuff? At your age, still might be possible."

I laughed. "Yes sir. I may hide a few things from myself. Can't tell if I'm hiding them or just not smart enough to turn them loose."

He paused before talking. "That's interesting," he said. "Not often I meet a deep-thinking man like myself."

I leaned against the truck. "What do you think it takes to make a man think deep?" I asked.

He resumed petting the dog. "Oh, that's easy," he said. "Hurt makes us search for answers. Ain't never a deep thought come out of happy times unless it started with some pain. Man has to hurt to prosper," he said.

"Hurt might just make him mean," I said. "And not prosper."

"True statement, but that comes from the character of the man, whether he can turn hurt into good or bad," he said.

"What's your name?" I asked.

"I'm George Acree," he said.

"How old are you?" I asked.

"Ninety-two," he said. "I think. I tend to get my even years mixed up."

"You live close by?" I asked.

"Yes. Up on Bobcat Crossing. Retired here ten years ago," he said.

"You worked until you were eighty-two?"

"Yes. Figured I'd quit, while I still have some productive years left," he said with a smile.

I laughed out loud. "What did you do?"

"Can you keep a secret?" he asked.

"Sure."

"I've got everybody fooled around here. Love this country dialect and easy life style. Should have done it fifty years ago, instead of teach seminary," he said.

I paused in disbelief. "Where did you teach?"

He looked embarrassed. "Vanderbilt," he said.

"So you're a doctor," I said.

"Of Philosophy," he said. "You know Ph.D-type doctor."

I said nothing, gathering my thoughts. The silence didn't seem to bother him at all. I sat on the tailgate. "Well, Mr. George Acree, can I ask you a Ph.D-type question?"

"Sure," he said.

"What would make a man turn so dark he could lose all traces of goodness?"

He rubbed the dog's ears while he thought. "Only one thing I know of," he said. "Cause goodness beats darkness every time. And a little goodness can whip a whole bunch of darkness. The answer is... he never had any goodness to lose."

"Is that possible?" I asked.

"Yes. Very rare. But entirely possible," he said. "Why do you ask?"

"I don't know," I said. "One of those things you ask yourself while driving down the road."

He looked at me with skepticism. "Come visit," he said. We'll finish this and maybe you can turn it loose."

"I'll keep your secret," I said.

"Good," he said. "And I'll return the favor some day."

In the afternoon, as the sun met the tree line, Taylor and Julia climbed the rock steps to my cabin while I nursed my first drink of the day at the porch table. They had walked the path through the woods and circled the house, causing the ugly dog to bark at their arrival.

Julia looked nervous, but for the first time I saw that she was very attractive. She had dark, thick hair and deep blue eyes when she looked at me and tried to smile.

"That's a strange looking dog," she said. "She has a nose mane, like a horse mane on the sides of her nose. And eyebrows like an old man."

"But she's a sweetie, aren't you Berit?" Taylor said rubbing behind the dog's ears.

"Y'all sit down," I said. "Get you something?"

"Whatever you're drinking is fine," Taylor said. "And I'll get it."

"Julia?"

"No. I'm fine," she said as Taylor disappeared into the cabin.

"You nervous?" I asked.

"A little," she said.

"Why?"

She grimaced. "The whole thing...."

"Do I make you nervous?" I asked.

"No, I mean, a little, the badge and everything," she said. "But for an older guy, you're way cool."

I smiled at her. "Thanks, I think. You haven't done anything wrong, have you?" I asked.

"No. I mean I sprayed him with pepper juice and that made him want to kill me, I guess. That could be wrong if he hurts me," she said. "Or just stupid."

"It's never stupid to protect yourself," I said. "Ever."

She relaxed for the first time as Taylor joined us with her drink. "So, you guys okay?" she said.

"Oh yeah," I said. "She thinks I'm old and 'way cool'."

"Anybody over thirty is old to Julia," Taylor said.

"Well, things change, Julia. I promise you'll see. But for now, I need to know everything Spike did or said to you that day. It's important because when we go to trial, all that will come out in your testimony."

"I have to testify?" she asked.

"Yes, you do, but just as background for the incident that occurred here."

"You mean when you slapped him around?"

"No," I said. "When he assaulted me for not doing what I asked and I arrested him."

Her eyes got bigger and she shook her head like she understood. "I see," she said.

"So, what did he do to you?" I asked.

"He followed me for a long time, you know, like right on my bumper and then passed me and slowed down and every time I'd try to pass, he'd block the road. So, I decided to just stop and go the other direction, but when I slowed, so did he and then I found a little farm road and I pulled into it to turn around, but he backed up and blocked me in. I couldn't go forward because of a gate."

"And what happened then?" I asked.

"He came up to my window and I was mad. I said what are you doing and you're in big trouble if you don't leave me alone and he just laughed and said I should get out and we could go into the woods. And I laughed at that and he reached into the window to touch me and I slapped his arm and sprayed him."

"What'd he do?"

"He covered his eyes and started screaming 'Bitch. I'll kill you,' and then he fell in a ditch and I got out and jumped in his truck and moved it cause he left the keys in it. And I left him running circles in the road. That's when I called Taylor and came here."

The sound of popping gravel interrupted our talk and a white Dodge truck came into our view, headed toward the cabin. It stopped and John Russell got out.

"Who is that?" Julia asked me, but was looking at John.

"A friend," I said.

John walked to the porch steps and stopped. He briefly looked at my dog and then back to me. "I'm sorry," he said. "I shouldn't have come without calling. W.B. told me where you live and I was in the area. "

"There's an extra chair up here, John. Come sit," I said. "We're just relaxing." I looked at Taylor and she was looking at Julia whose eyes wouldn't leave John. He climbed the steps and stopped at the table.

"Meet Miss Taylor James and Julia, I'm sorry, I haven't heard your last name," I said.

"Spencer," Julia announced. "Hi, John, I'm Julia Spencer."

Taylor extended her hand and John took it. "Ma'am," he said. "Julia." He scooted the chair from the table and sat, looking uncomfortable.

"Relax, John," I said. "We're just talking. You're not interrupting anything."

He placed his hands on the table and crossed his fingers and looked at me. "I just wanted to say thanks for your help. I'm not used to strangers being so…" And he couldn't say the right word.

"You didn't have to drive all the way over here to thank me," I said.

"No sir. That's not quite right," he said. "I did. You seemed to care about what happened the other night, the truth I mean."

"I do care, John. You see, you and me are attached. That's the way good things happen. I didn't know you before a couple of days ago, but W.B. does. And I care about him and he cares about you, so that means I care about you," I said.

John looked embarrassed.

"What's wrong?" Julia asked across the table.

John looked at her and then back at me. "I didn't know men talked like that," he said. "No offense."

"Most men don't," Taylor said. "Somehow, he gets away with it."

I smiled.

"Yeah, right before he slaps some thug on the ear so hard he can't get up," Julia smiled.

John smiled back at her. "Sometimes, it's necessary to get a bad man's full attention."

"Oh, Mr. Stewart got his attention," Julia said smiling.

Taylor was looking at me across the table and cut her eyes toward Julia. "Julia, why don't you take John and feed the horses and dogs," she said. "That has to be done before supper. You are staying to eat with us, John."

"No ma'am," he said. "I just came to say my thanks."

"Have you got some place you have to be?" Taylor asked.

"Well, no ma'am, but…"

"No buts," Taylor said. "You are eating with us, provided you earn your way by helping Julia feed. You have a problem with eating with us? Don't forget, we're attached."

"No ma'am."

"No what? You won't eat with us or you don't have a problem?" Taylor asked.

For the first time John smiled comfortably, figuring the playfulness of Taylor James. "No ma'am, I don't have a problem helping Julia and I don't have a problem eating with you. I'd appreciate it."

"She likes to banter," I said to John.

"Can we take your truck?" Julia asked.

"Sure," John said. "Let's go. Uh…what kind of dog is that?" he asked.

"Ugly," I said.

"Ain't no such thing as an ugly dog," he said. "And that dog looks real smart."

"Smarter than me, probably," I said.

And John turned to walk down the steps and Julia followed, then turned to us, her back to John, and mouthed to Taylor. "Thank you."

We heard the truck doors shut and the white Dodge backed out of the driveway. Taylor looked at me and smiled. "So, what can you cook for the kids?"

I stared at her. "Was it you who invited John to eat with us?"

"Yes," she said. "I believe it was."

"So, you invited them to eat my cooking?"

She smiled. "Yes, I believe I did. Is there a problem?"

"No. No problem at all, if you can do some really simple things to help. I'm sure I'll come up with something fun," I said.

"Like what?"

"You can boil water, can't you?"

She smirked.

"How 'bout find me four zip-lock bags. Can you do that? Pour shredded cheese into a bowl? Or chop onions and green peppers? Any of those suit you?"

"I can get them all done. No problem," she said.

"Good. I'll do all the rest," I said.

We smiled at each other across the table. I knew she was playing and she knew I was playing and it was fun, like way back in time when life allowed the present to dominate all your feelings and there were few worries about tomorrow or regrets about yesterday.

"By the way, we are attached?" I asked. "You said we were attached."

"When did I say that?"

"To John. You said, 'Don't forget. We're attached.'"

"Do you remember exact words all the time?" she asked.

"Yes. I do. Exact words. It's a gift," I said smiling.

"Are you ever wrong, because I don't remember saying that," she said, looking away.

"Deception. It's all over your face. You said it. You know you said it, and now you're afraid to admit it," I said.

"Actually, I did, but not in the way you said. I was talking to John and when I said 'we're attached' I meant John and I are attached," she said. "'We're attached' was John and me, not you and me."

"And when, I might ask, did you get attached to John, seeing as today is the first time you've ever seen him?"

"Are you interrogating me?" she asked.

"I'm interviewing you. Had I placed you under arrest, then I'd be interrogating you," I said.

"I see," she said. "Then let me be clear." And she looked straight at me. "I became attached to John Russell the night you sat bare-footed on my porch and told me about a young man who tries to make sense of a life torn by a dying mother and a dead father and a shoe box full of honor. That's when I became attached to him."

I let that sink in. "So I ask you again. Are we attached? And let me be clear. I'm talking about you and me."

"What do you think?" she asked.

"I think there's great potential," I said.

"And I think it's great fun finding potential," she said. "So you gonna cook or what?"

CHAPTER 14

Julia and John came in the house laughing. Her dark hair was wet, as was her blouse and John was doing his best to tone her down, but happiness is hard to contain and Julia Spencer was very happy. They entered the kitchen, where Taylor sat with a drink at the table and I stood at the sink sipping mine.

"Look what he did to me," she said laughing.

John looked embarrassed again. "I had nothing to do with her getting soaked," he said. "She asked me to turn the water on and I did. You know filling the horse tank?"

Taylor smiled. "I know the horse tank, John," she said.

"Well, I didn't…couldn't know that the nozzle was barely attached and when the pressure hit it, it flew off spewing water everywhere," he said.

Julia pulled a rubber band from her hip pocket, pulled her thick hair backwards and bound a long pony tail. "There, all fixed," she said.

"Can you fry bacon?" I asked John.

"Well, yes sir," he said.

"There's some bacon," I said pointing to the counter. "And there's the skillet on the stove. Let's get to frying."

John removed his hat and moved to the sink, washing his hands. I handed him a towel. "I like clean hands," I said. "You passed the first test."

"Am I being tested?" he said.

"When you are with him, you are always being tested," Taylor said looking in my direction.

"Is that a bad thing? Life is a test," I said.

"Not sure about that," she said. She turned to Julia. "Can you boil water?"

Julia smirked at her exactly the way Taylor had smirked at me. "Where's the pot?" she said. "I'm all over this test thing. I can boil some water. Known throughout the country for my water-boiling skills. Move over Cowboy, and share the stove." She nudged John sideways with her hip. John looked embarrassed again, but smiled.

I watched them all in this backwoods kitchen so far away from my home in Nashville. For a split second, I felt guilty for being here, and then it went away. Julia was happy. I looked at Taylor and she was happy. If I had a mirror, I think I could have seen myself happy. And without seeing his face, I knew John Russell's heart was beating very fast, standing so close to this young girl who boiled water with pride.

"How old are you, Julia?" I asked.

Julia looked over her shoulder at me. "Just turned eighteen last month," she said.

John looked at her. "Me, too," he said.

"When?" she said.

"The seventh," he said.

Her eyes got big and then she turned to Taylor and back to John. "Mine's the eighth," she said. "We were born one day apart!"

"Well, I knew I was older," he said seriously. "The water will be boiling long before the bacon is ready," he said. "You might want to turn that thing down a bit."

"Don't tell me how to boil water," she said laughing.

"Okay," I said. "If you two will quit arguing for just a second. Here's the game plan. It's called game warden omelets. It's called game warden omelets because we needed a quick way to fix breakfast on the tailgate of a truck, with no mess to clean up. When John gets the bacon cooked and Taylor puts cheese in a bowl and chops some onions and peppers, we take two eggs and break them into a zip-lock bag and squish them up real good and then add whatever you want in your omelet to the bag, seal it, and drop in the boiling water that Julia has expertly prepared. Seven minutes later, remove the bag and inside will be the finest omelet you ever tasted. Empty the water, throw away the bags and you're through."

Taylor was smiling now. "And that means you will have done absolutely nothing to prepare this meal," she said.

"I said I would come up with something," I said. "Never said I'd cook it."

"Neither did I," she said. "Julia, while you're waiting for the water to boil, how 'bout doing that cheese thing and chop up that stuff he said?"

John leaned toward Julia at the stove and whispered in her ear. We couldn't hear, but Julia turned to Taylor and said yes, ma'am, so I assumed his message had something to do with not arguing.

"One more thing," I said. "Proper meal preparation involves dumping the stress of the day. Taylor and I are having a drink while we watch you guys cook. You, too, may have a glass of wine if you like because in my house, if you're old enough to fight and die for your country, you're old enough to drink responsibly. So, would you like a glass of wine while you cook?"

Taylor stood and crossed the room standing next to me. She stood on tip-toes and whispered in my ear. "You know what, it's still my house."

"Technically," I whispered back to her. "You can't enter this house without my permission; therefore, it's my house while I pay rent."

"Uh uh," Julia said. "No whispering."

"I'm sorry, but John started it. John, didn't you do the whisper thing just a few minutes ago?" Taylor asked.

"Yes ma'am," he said while turning the bacon. "I was giving Julia some wise advice."

Julia immediately whispered something to John while hiding her mouth with her hand. John, in turn, cleared his throat and said nothing.

"I would love some wine," Julia then said. "What goes best with eggs? Red or white?"

"Red, "I said. What do you think, Taylor?"

She paused. "Technically, it's white, but in the country those rules are suspended because common sense takes over."

"Common sense is a wonderful thing," I said.

"There you go, kids," she said.

"I don't understand," Julia said. "What are you talking about?"

Taylor smiled. "John? Got a theory about what I'm talking about?"

"No offense, but y'all passed me about ten minutes ago," he said.

Taylor drank from her glass and paused. Then she smiled at me. "He has no white wine," she said.

I sipped the bourbon and it burned going down. I suddenly wanted to move away from her, but figured it would show defeat, so I stayed put.

I went to the cabinet and pulled out a Merlot, uncorked it, and poured Julia a glass. I turned to John and motioned with the bottle.

"No thanks," he said. "I don't drink."

"Why?" I asked.

"I don't like drunks," he said.

"I don't either" I said. "Having a glass of wine does not make a drunk."

"All I know is that if I don't drink, I'll never get drunk," he said.

"Well, I can't argue with that logic," I said. "But you'll also never know the experience of sharing a good wine with friends. Just something to think about. Let's cook game warden omelets."

Later, after the perfect omelets fell out of the bags onto our plates, with all the "stuff" miraculously inside, and we talked about stubborn horses and good dogs and needed rain and favorite lines from good movies, Julia and John moved to the front porch to listen to barred owls calling in the woods nearby. Taylor washed the one dirty skillet, plates and glasses like she had always planned that job. And I watched her move at the sink.

"I don't plan everything as much as you think," I said.

She turned to face me, drying a glass. "Really," she said.

"Really. Everything is not a test. Not here. Not with you. Sometimes I just want to know what you think about things," I said.

She looked away. "I'm not used to that," she said. "Someone wanting to know what I think."

"I do," I said.

"Why?"

"There is no why," I said. "I just do. Maybe you can explain it, but I can't."

"So, what do you want to know?" she asked.

"About a million things," I said. "Maybe we'll have time, but who really knows."

"Start now," she said.

"Okay. What do you do? I mean work-wise. I've wanted to know that for a while."

"I buy and sell books," she said. "My father owned a book distribution company. I run it now. About a hundred book stores in the south."

"You can do all that from your house?" I asked.

"Modern technology," she said. "Ain't it something? And I dabble in collectible books, you know, find first editions of rare titles and resell them to collectors."

"And then there are the horses and dogs," I said.

"No money there," she said. "Just enjoyment."

"What do you think about those two on the front porch?" I asked.

She placed the glass in the cabinet and started drying another one. "I've never seen her like this," she said. "She took to him, like immediately. Julia's dated some guys and one was kind of serious last year, but I've never seen her light up like this. What do you think?"

I toyed with an ink pen on the table, switching its ends against the wood. "I think he's never had a night like tonight. I think he is happy and scared and very confused. I keep reminding myself that he's totally without blood relatives and his closest friend is dying and when I think about his future, I guess I just wanted to say thanks to you and Julia for tonight. I think it has given him a view of a future he never thought possible."

"I want to hire him," she said bluntly. "To help around the farm. I told you that Julia is pretty much estranged from her parents and I'm all she has and to be frank, we need him to help with heavy stuff."

"I don't think he could afford the commute for what you would pay him," I said.

"He wouldn't have to," she said. "There is a small guest cottage behind the barn. He could move here and finish school here. If things continue like I saw tonight, he and Julia could drive to school every day together."

I looked up at her. "You would do that?"

"Sure, and be happy about it," she said. "It would make everyone happy, I think. Don't you?"

I paused, and then decided to be truthful. "I like the idea, cause I can't be here all the time. And I trust John to look out for you two. He's good at that sort of thing and there ain't no 'back up' in him." She looked at me with a question that never came out. "I had a talk with Tiller Mabry."

"Is he still alive?" she asked. "After you talked?"

"Very much," I said. "Not sure I've ever met anyone that impressed me with such pure evil. And I'll tell you, Taylor, I've met some real losers in my life."

"Seems like I tried to warn you," she said. "But why do you worry about Julia and me?"

"He mentioned you. That's why. By name. And what bothered me was it was said in a way that he thought you meant something to me. How could he know that?"

She paused. "Know what?"

I smiled. "That we are connected."

"Maybe he doesn't," she said. "Maybe he just knew that you were here when you arrested Spike and assumed you knew us."

"Maybe," I said. "But I would still feel better with John around."

"What did he say about us," she asked.

I paused. "I can't remember," I said. "Just something about Spike and Julia and you and him."

"Don't lie to me," she said. "You remember discussions exactly. That's what you said."

"It's just talk," I said. "His words were to get a response from me."

"And did you respond?" she asked.

"Yes. I said I would pray for him," I said.

She looked perplexed. "Pray for him?" she asked.

I paused again, having ventured into an arena I was unprepared to explain. "Yes," I said.

"Explain," she said.

"Can't. Not now," I said. "Just remember, we've got lots to find out about each other. I would bet that it'll take awhile to understand all the deepest parts."

"Maybe," she said. "Maybe it will go quicker than you think. So, have you?" she asked.

"Have I what?"

"Prayed for him."

"No," I said. "I haven't."

She put the glass away and turned back to me. Then she looked toward the porch. "Well, what do you think they're doing?"

I noticed the abrupt change in subject matter. "Looking for potential, I'd say."

"At that age, you don't look for it," she said. "It overwhelms you."

"How long has it been since you've been overwhelmed," I asked.

"Oh, about a week," she said. "You?"

"Well," I said. "As soon as my mind clears from the vision of you standing there in those jeans, I'll answer that question. The memory of you during the day makes me happy inside."

Taylor moved to the table, pulled out a chair and sat across from me. She stared at me and then laid her head on her hands like she was resting from something tiring. Her eyes were not on me, but somewhere else across the room. "Please tell me what that means. What possible memory of me could cause you to be happy?"

"Look at me," I said.

"No," she said. "Looking at you will mess it up."

"Okay," I said. But I didn't say anything for a long time. "Sometimes I feel totally vulnerable with you, and it doesn't scare me."

She didn't say anything for a long time. "And that makes you happy?"

"No. The fact that I am not scared of being vulnerable scares the hell out of me. It's the memory of you that makes me happy."

"See, that makes no sense to me," she said.

I took her hand away from her face. "Look at me," I said. "Do you believe me?"

She raised her head. "Yes."

"Then don't worry about understanding it," I said. "Just know it."

"Okay," she said finally. She looked toward the porch again. "Wonder if they're having a meaningful conversation out there like we are in here?"

"Meaningful? They could be counting in Spanish to each other and it would be meaningful," I said. "I'll talk to him about the job, if you want me to."

"Yeah. See what he says."

"Are you okay?" I asked.

"Yeah, I'm good," she said.

She held my eyes in hers for a long time, but there were no words. I heard a barred owl call outside and then we heard them laughing on the porch. Taylor smiled, like the sounds of their voices had cured something painful and I wished I could understand why she questioned her presence could be anything but good for my spirit. It was then that I realized the imperfection of the human language: that words were not adequate for messages of the heart and the confusion is in the infancy of our ability to trust communication without words. We seem to demand that those feelings be backed by words that validate our feelings, when it should be the other way…our feelings should clarify our imperfect words.

CHAPTER 15

The following night, W.B and I watched the entrance of the Ridge Runner Club from across the road under some heavy-branched pine trees. We had been observing the beer joint since dark.

"So, you think the boy was happy?" he asked.

"Well, you know him better, but I think so," I said.

"I told him to take the deal," he said. "He's so broke it's hard for him to pay attention, and the house is nothing but memories of his mom. He needs a new look at life, cause I'm the only thing left there for him and, well, you know how long I'm gonna last."

"No, I don't. You could be around for a long time." I paused. "Changing schools didn't bother him?" I asked.

"Naw," he said as he lit another cigarette. He can still see his friends. We're not talking thirty miles distance."

"It could be dangerous, W.B. We're kind of putting him in the middle of this thing, you know," I said.

"I will guarandamtee you that John Russell is up to it. You ain't never seen the boy fight, but I want to tell you, I'd hate to fight him, and you know I'd fight King Kong if'n the son of a bitch was still alive," he said smiling.

"Please tell me you know that King Kong was not real," I said.

W.B. looked at me and a smiled. "Oh, he's real," he said. "Just not quite the way it was in the movie."

We didn't say anything for a long time. We sat there in that truck watching a lonely road and waiting for headlights. "So," I said after a while. "How are you feeling?"

"You mean the cancer?"

"I guess," I said. "Any pain?"

"Pain's a relative thing, I reckon," he said.

"Explain," I said.

"That's a hard one," he said. "I guess there's more pain in not looking forward to anything. Life hurts when the only thing to look forward to is the end of it."

"Maybe it's not the end," I said. "Maybe it's just a change."

He looked at me across the dark cab. "Now, you ain't gonna go get religious on me, are ya?"

"Call it what you like," I said. "When I was five, I stuck a big splinter in my thumb running my hand down a split rail fence. One of those big wooden toothpick type splinters and it hurt like hell and I remember the blood was deep red and I was scared and I wanted it out and cried. My father came over, looked at the thing, jerked it out and said, 'It's nothing son…quit crying and go on.'

What if dying is just like that splinter and all this worrying over dying is nothing and we go on?"

"I won't spend one night in the hospital," he said. "Not one. I ain't ending it in a white room."

"That wasn't the point," I said.

"I know what your point was," he said. "God's gonna pluck that big ol'cancer splinter out of me."

"Nope," I said. "Don't believe that at all. I believe you're gonna die…sometime anyway. My point was that as soon as my father walked up to me, I wasn't scared anymore. I knew he was going to fix it. And he did. That's my point."

"You had faith in your old man," he said. "That's your point?"

"Yep. That's it. Just wondering if you got any faith in our old man?"

"If he's there, then he knows me real good. And he knows why I done everything I've done and I don't have a problem being judged, if that answers your question," he said.

"Kind of," I said.

"I'm leaving everything to John, except the rifle I promised you. Help the boy get an education, maybe," he said. "Make sure he gets it."

"I will," I said. "And you've got nothing to look forward to?"

He looked at me again. "Well, there's one thing," he said. "Keeps me going every day."

"And that would be?" I asked.

"None of your damned business," he said.

It was ten o' clock when the two men arrived. The driver was tall and lanky with a blonde braid that hung to the small of his back, and the passenger was short and stumpy with tats across his upper arms that resembled briars, like Jesus wore on his head. Modern night vision equipment is truly amazing.

"You ready for this?" I asked W.B.

"I was born ready," he said. "Hope these boys are smart." And we exited the vehicle and made our way across the dark pasture to the parking lot.

I opened the bar door and stepped inside. There were eight or ten people drinking long necks at the bar and most of the tables were full. I quickly scanned the room and found most of the eyes were on me. W.B. had my back. A Lyle Lovett song was playing through the smoke and muffled conversations. But the talk quickly subsided and Lyle's voice was all alone.

I decided to get on with it. "Hate to interrupt you folks, but we're looking for Hank Smothers and Tom Smithy," I said loudly.

Silence.

W.B. walked around me, wandered through the tables to the back where our boys were sitting. He looked down at them. "Get up and walk out," he said. "Now."

The longhair looked up at him. "Fuck you," he said taking a drink from the bottle. W.B didn't show any emotion at all and simply reached down, grabbed the braid, pulling the man from the chair and dragging him across the floor toward the door. The burly guy came after his friend until I stopped him half way. W.B. and I stood back to back in the middle of the bar. The long-hair tried to get up, but W.B. jerked his head downward, slamming his face into the floor. "Don't move, Hank" W.B. said. "I'd hate to scalp your ass in front of all these fine people."

Tom swung at me. It was a round house move that I saw coming, so I simply stepped back a half a step and let his momentum carry him around. I stepped forward, did a leg sweep and took him down among tables and chairs and bottles crashing to the floor. "Don't move," I said with my knee and two hundred pounds of weight on his neck. "Put your hands behind you." He did. And I handcuffed the burly man and stood him up. We moved toward the door with our prisoners amongst stares and whispers.

Tiller Mabry was standing at the door smiling. "Well, well," he said. "The carp cops have arrived to harass hard-working country folks."

"Is that what you are?" I asked. "Hard-working country boy?"

"Well, sure," he said. "Why don't you let those boys be? They ain't done nothin' cept try to have a cool drink of beer with friends."

"If that was true," I said. "I don't believe I'd have these warrants in my pocket for their arrest. Move away from the door, Tiller."

"I tell you what. I got five hundred dollars for any man who whips this carp cop's ass right now," he announced to the crowd.

I pushed Tom against the wall. "Stay," I said like addressing a dog. And I moved to the bar. W.B. stood against the wall still holding Hank by the hair, staring at Tiller. Tom suddenly made a quick move for the door and W.B. hit him with a straight right to the gut, at which time Tom promptly vomited into the wall.

"Why, Tom," W.B. said casually, "You've come unfed."

After a second, I said, "Anybody in here so hard-up for money that you'll follow the coward, Tiller Mabry's play?"

There was silence as eyes moved around the room watching for a taker. "Maybe," a deep voice came from the back of the bar. And a tall man about thirty walked forward. He wore a John Deere cap and a knife-scar across his cheek."

"What's your name?" I asked.

"Harold," he said.

"Well, Harold, if it's worth five hundred, come on, but here's what's gonna happen. I'm gonna hurt you. I'm not gonna whip you. I'm gonna hurt you. And then I'm gonna arrest you. And then you're gonna go to jail and use the five hundred to make your bond. And then I'm gonna arrest the coward Tiller Mabry for inciting a fight. So, I really don't care, one way or the other, but you need to know what's gonna happen."

"Or maybe," Tiller said with a quivering lip. "He breaks your fucking legs. And ties them in a knot. And you don't arrest nobody cause you figured it not worth the effort. That could happen."

"Wanna bet?" I heard W.B. say. And everyone turned to the wall. "I'll bet your life against mine that that won't happen."

Now I had a problem. I looked at W.B. and tried to give him a "be cool" look, but it didn't take. And from experience, there was no turning him off.

Tiller paused, looking at W.B. "This fight ain't with you," he said.

"It is now," W.B. said flatly. "You bet five hundred dollars. That ain't much to prove a man's worth. Bet me your life. There ain't three men in here working together that can whup his ass much less break his legs. If they do, I'll let you shoot me, and if you ain't got the grit to shoot me, I'll fuckin' shoot myself. But if Ethan wins the fight, I break your filthy, cowardly, shit-streaked neck, or I'll let you kill yourself, if that suits you better. How 'bout it? Wanna play?"

The room was silent. Tiller stared at W.B. I turned to Harold. "How 'bout it, Harold?" I asked. "You still game?"

"I'm waiting for Tiller," he said.

I turned to Tiller. He tried to smile, but it didn't work. "Hell, I just met those boys anyway. It ain't like they're family," he said. "We'll pass this time," he said.

I turned back to Harold. He said nothing, so I moved through the tables and stood facing him. I stuck out my hand. "No hard feelings," I said.

He looked at my hand and shook it. His grip was strong. "Same here," he said. And I moved away from him toward the door, where W.B. waited, holding our prisoners.

As I passed Tiller at the bar, I quickly reached out and grabbed his head pulling it to mine. He fought for a second before I whispered in his ear. "I forgive you." He jerked away and spat on the floor.

"Fuck you, you som bitch," he slurred.

I smiled at him. "Have a nice night, Tiller." And we left the bar, leading our boys though the dark parking lot.

"What about our truck?" Hank asked.

"We'll have it towed to the jail," I said.

I turned to see several people spilling out into the parking lot to watch.

"Where we gonna get," Tom asked. "You're driving a damn pick up."

"You think this is Melvin Metro work here, boy?" W.B. said. "Hell, yore in the country. You ride in the bed." And we handcuffed them to the tool box in the back of W.B.'s truck and took off, leaving a crowd in the parking lot looking on and starting stories that would last a long while.

After five miles we figured we weren't being followed and Hank beat on the rear window with his foot. W.B. rolled his window down and slowed.

"Stop the damn truck, W.B.," he yelled.

"Not yet," W.B. yelled back.

And we took a right turn on a gravel road and then another on a logging road and drove a mile through the woods to a deserted, dark cabin. W.B. killed the engine and opened the door, flooding light to the bed. He lowered the tailgate and stepped up, as the two boys looked at him.

"W.B., you better not take these cuffs off cause I'm gonna come after you," Tom said. "You had no right to gut punch me."

W.B. smiled and loosened Tom's chains. "Hell, Tom, I mean, Bill, that was just for show. Sorry if it hurt," he said. "You hungry?"

"Kiss my ass," he said. "You watch Ethan? Now there's a man who can do it right. Swept my legs and we broke a few tables. That's a show. Not abuse."

"Aw shut up, Bill," the long haired man said. "He damn near pulled all my hair out and you don't hear me complaining. We need to talk and get the hell out of here," he said.

I leaned against the bed. "You boys did real good back there," I said. "What did you find out in a week?"

"More than I figured we'd get," Sam, the long hair, said. "We got cameras at his house and a daily log of vehicles coming and going. We got everybody who has come and gone in seven days. We got one trip to Nashville and a meeting with a lawyer, named Steve Turrin, and another grease ball driving a car with Michigan tags. Hadn't got a name yet on him, but he's got prison tats and looks bad news. We got a girl that stays with Mabry most of the time. She's rough looking but a body that won't quit and she drives a dented red mustang with Montgomery County plates. Registration is to a Shelia Barnes."

"Was she there tonight?" I asked.

"Yep," Tom said. "She was in the corner watching and I'd bet she had a gun on you the whole time. She had her hands in her lap under a coat and never took her eyes off you."

"I had her," W.B. said.

"Bullshit," Tom said. "You were too busy beatin' on me and Sam."

"She wore a red tank top," W.B. said. "She had a tattoo on her left shoulder, a nail or something, and she was cool as hell, but she wasn't watching Ethan so much as Tiller. And when Tiller would throw his eyes to another guy, a older guy in a blue shirt two tables over from her, she would watch that guy and when she watched that guy, she weren't cool no more. She got nervous. He was the one with the gun, I'd say."

"Enough," I said. "Good stuff, but I need two things. When's the best time to catch Tiller at his house? And is there any place he goes regularly that I can find him every day?"

"He gets cigarettes or coffee at Hank's Market every day about one or two. He don't get up till late cause he don't go to bed 'til daylight. Stays out all night…every night. And the only time to guarantee he's home is Friday afternoon. Seems to be a staging area for the weekends' activities."

"How many people stay at his house?" I asked.

"Depends," Tom said. "On whether he's dealing drugs or guns or making deals on this year's paddlefish eggs. He's trying to set up his fishermen now for this winter's harvest. Season starts November 15th."

"On the average, how many there on Friday afternoon?" I asked.

"Him, the girl, four brothers, and assorted other girls and two or three more muscle guys. I'd say count on ten."

"Thanks," I said. "I owe you boys. How long can you stick around?"

"I got to leave tomorrow afternoon for three days," Sam said. "Got a bear deal in the mountains that has to go down day after tomorrow. Tom can stay for a while. McEllis said your deal is number one after the bear buy."

"Okay," I said. "Let's get you back to your other vehicle and we'll take care of the truck. You can pick it up tomorrow morning. And remember, we took you to jail in Nashville, not here. We got the paper work to back it up in case he checks."

"You boys friendly with him at all?" W.B. asked.

"No," Tom said. "He's just seen us at the bar every night. We sold him some bootlegged Crown, but he passed on the snakes. Looked at us like we were crazy. He's scary smart, Chief. You better watch this one."

"I ain't the Chief anymore," I said. "Don't call me that. McEllis is the man, now."

"Funny," Sam said. "McEllis still calls you Chief and he's the Chief."

"Habit," I said. "That's all. Let's get." And we loaded up and drove out through the darkness of the April backwoods along Kentucky Lake without saying another word.

I looked at my watch as we bounced the rough roads. Ten fifty-five. I wondered what Taylor was doing right now. I wished I knew what she was thinking right now. I wished I knew what the sinking feeling was in my gut, but I knew if I was with her it would go away.

CHAPTER 16

At one the next afternoon, I pulled into the parking area of Hank's Market. It was a typical country store with a gravel parking area and oil stains on the ground and paper wrappers everywhere. Pickups and old cars surrounded the store. Tiller was on the front porch watching, opening a pack of cigarettes. I walked up the steps to the store and he turned to look at me.

"You following me?" he said throwing the wrapper to the ground.

I leaned against a paint-scarred steel pole supporting the front porch. "Just lucky timing, I'd say."

He lit the cigarette and blew the smoke upwards. "It ain't never lucky timing for you to run into me," he said.

"I'm curious," I said. "Why do you hate me? I've never done anything to you except talk. Where does that come from, all that hate?"

An old man came out the front door, looked at us quickly and hurried off the porch, staring with a bent neck all the way to his truck.

"Why don't we move to the table," he said, motioning with his head to a picnic area off to the side of the store. "Seeing as you're getting all religious on me again."

"Sure," I said. "I'll follow you."

He smiled. "Sure thing, Carp Cop. What? You afraid I'll shoot you in the back?"

"No," I said. "I doubt if you're even carrying a gun. Are you?"

He moved off the porch toward the table and spoke to the air in front of him. "Never can tell these days, can you? I noticed you ain't totin' a gun these days. Didn't have one the last night, but you had that other crazy Carp Cop with you. You ain't got him around today and you still ain't totin' a gun."

"Changed my views on things over the years," I said. "Don't reckon I need one anymore."

"You gonna talk 'em to death?" he asked.

"No, I just don't worry about dying much," I said. "Do you?"

"Damn right, I do," he said. "I ain't through having fun fuckin' with people like you. Keeps me wanting to breathe every day, so I can show up the do-gooders of the world.

We sat at the table across from one another, our elbows resting on the old knife-scarred wood.

"You gotta tape recorder running?" he asked.

"Nope."

"Would you tell me if you did," he asked.

"Sure."

"Sure you would," he said. "Don't matter to me anyway. I got nothing to hide."

"Yes, you do," I said. "And it's hurting you inside. You're hiding your whole life."

His lip quivered, but he stayed calm. "See, that's what I hate about you. You think you know me. And you don't know shit."

"I know about hiding stuff," I said. "We all do."

"Maybe what you hide makes me stronger. Maybe I like the shit you hate. Ever think of that, Possum Sheriff?"

His eyes were suddenly stronger…almost happy.

"I have," I said. "Studied on that very thing the other day. Doesn't make any sense, though. Cause if that's the case, then wrong would be as strong as right. And trust me. Good beats bad every time in the end."

He laughed out loud and I noticed his yellowed teeth. "Trust you?" he said. "For what? To teach me right from wrong?" He laughed again. "Ain't nothin' in life but what is. And here's what is…now listen real careful, Carp Cop, so you'll remember it when it happens. It makes me so happy to tell you this…I figured out a way for you to die and there ain't nothin' nobody can do to stop me or get me because of it." He paused looking at me and then slapped me on the shoulder. "Ain't that great!"

I leaned closer to him and whispered. "Come on, if you can't be stopped and nobody can get you for it, then tell me how it's going to happen. Just between you and me. Is it the same way you had Samuel killed? Is it that brilliant? Cause we know how you did that. We know everything. Everything, Tiller. The last detail."

He smiled again. "I think I'm a free man." He looks around. "Yeah, I believe I'm free and nobody is after me. Court says I'm free. But you." he whispered. "This is much better than that. This is much better cause you're gonna cause it with your own smart-ass ways. Your own so-called goodness which I think is total bullshit, is going to kill you. See, you're actually gonna kill yourself."

His words slammed my consciousness and I struggled to recover. "Really?" I said.

"Really," he said. "And then I'm gonna hurt everyone you care about after you're dead. Remember that."

"That's not a problem," I lied, slipping quickly into some law enforcement survival dialogue that was now second nature to me. "I don't care about anybody right now except you. I care about you. I want you to confess and have a life that means something good. You can do it, Tiller. You can beat this thing. Just confess."

"Confess to who?" he asked. "You? I don't owe you shit. You're no better'n me, you badge-wearing prick. Fuck you and your confessions." And his lip had lost control and his face was jerking in rage and redness and the spit gathered at the corner of his mouth and his tongue was thick with anger.

And his anger gave me strength. "I don't need your confession," I said. "I am no better than you. We agree. But God needs you to confess to help yourself."

He stood abruptly and looked down at me. "I'll love every second of this," he said. "You confess to your god and I'll shoot the shit with mine."

I stood and looked at him. "There. You said it and it didn't hurt you at all."

"What?"

"Love," I said. "Say it driving down the road. Say it before you sleep. It'll help."

He walked away laughing and I stood there watching, wanting to reach across the space between us and beat his face into bloody death, until it stared sleepy-eyed up at me and I could know he didn't exist in the world where I breathed. *Don't, Jesus* whispered. Rise above your anger. Find your other world and stay there.

I pulled the hidden microphone from my shirt as I got into the truck and then dialed the number. "You get it?" I asked.

"Yep," Tom whispered. "Got it all."

"Where's W.B.?" I asked.

"Not sure," he said. "Wouldn't tell me. He's a long way off, I know that."

"Where are you?" I asked.

"See the old farmer by the beat-to-shit Ford right in front of you?"

"Yeah," I said. The man was dirty and old and stabbing cans with a stick, throwing them in the back of his truck."

"That's me," he said waving slightly.

"These guys are good," I whispered, but not so he could hear.

CHAPTER 17

On the way home I took back roads, exploring new country, a meaningful aspect of the job. We drive thousands of miles learning the roads and where they go. Sometimes the best cases are made while cruising back roads and you have no particular agenda. Sometimes you don't make cases, but meet people that become meaningful in your life. When I turned onto Bobcat Crossing Road, I remembered the old man. After a while, I found his house.

The house was modest and was built about two hundred yards from the road on a hill. I saw him sitting on the ground under a big oak in the front yard. I couldn't pass him by. And when I left the vehicle to approach him, he never looked up, but got on his all-fours studying something on the ground.

"Mr. Acree," I said.

"Mr. Stewart," he said without looking up. "Ants are amazing, don't you think?"

I sat cross-legged on the ground and saw a column of ants making their way across the dirt in front of him. "I never really studied them," I said.

"Such intensity in their actions," he said. "Have you ever seen an ant that doesn't seem to know exactly where it's going?"

"It must be nice," I said.

He looked up at me for the first time and slowly moved to a sitting position. "These old bones," he said. "They move slow. So, you got a problem with where you're going?"

"Did I say that?" I asked.

"I believe you did," he said.

"You don't miss much, do you?"

"I don't miss anything," he said sincerely.

A breeze rattled last year's leaves above our heads, several releasing from the tree and drifting sideways to the ground. "I need to know if we can speak confidentially," I said. "Since you are a retired man of the cloth, could I fit into some type of guaranteed confidentiality?"

"Sure," he said. "I won't speak to another human being of anything you say."

"And why do I trust you?" I asked.

"Don't know," he said. "You may just be a great judge of character."

I smiled at him. "Okay," I said. "Tell me about vengeance. I've tried to beat it, but I'm afraid I've developed tunnel vision."

"And so go the ants," he said. "In a deliberate direction with no clue why."

I paused watching the ants. "Maybe it's that I can't see the problem while hoping for justice."

He picked a piece of grass from his pants and studied it. "Temporal or eternal justice?" he asked.

"What?"

"You want my thoughts? I have to know it what realm you want the answer. Earthly survival or eternal survival. Two realities. You can't have a foot in both worlds at the same time."

"I'm not sure," I said.

"Then you're an ant," he said. "Look. The human language isn't specific enough to describe a spiritual path. But we can use imperfect words that lead to perfect spiritual answers."

"I disagree," I said. "Good communicators could choose the right words."

"I see you have a wedding ring. Do you love your wife?" he asked.

I smiled again. "Yes," I said. "Very much."

He pulled a small writing pad from his shirt pocket and produced a small pen and with trembling fingers put pen to paper. "Okay," he said. "Describe your love for your wife. I'll just write it down."

I pondered, but remained silent.

"I thought you loved her," he said.

"I do."

"Then give me the words."

"She became a major part of me," I whispered.

"What part?"

"The good part."

"Well, maybe you could describe the good part. It would give me some idea of your love for her," he said.

"The part of me that is attached to something very good," I said.

"I see," he said while writing. "Your love for your wife is described as a major part of you that is attached to something very good. Hmmm. What is that something?"

"Okay, Mr. Acree," I said. " I think you know what I mean."

"Do I," he said with raised eyebrows. "I don't even know that you do love her."

"Well, I do," I said.

"Prove it," he said.

I looked at him quickly. "Have you been talking to my daughter?"

He smiled. "No, but I bet she's a real good daughter."

"I love my wife and that's all that counts," I said.

He leaned closer to me and lowered his voice for emphasis. "You can't prove it. You can tell me words that fit what we define as love, but no one can actually prove what it is here." And he touched my chest with a bony finger.

His touch was powerful somehow. I felt his energy. "I just came by for some advice," I said.

"And before I can help you, we have to establish an understanding of my words, so that when I can't get them exactly right, you will still know what counts."

I probed the ground with my finger and unearthed an acorn. "I understand," I said. "Help me. What are the problems with wanting justice?"

"Forget the problems," he said. "That's material talk. There's only choices. Some choices are painful and there is nothing but pain in the end. Other choices hurt, but are worth the pain. Kinda like spiritual aspirin."

"I don't like pain," I said. "It hurts."

"Supposed to," he said. "And that's a good thing."

"How?"

"It teaches us to judge the pain as worthy or not," he said. "Was the choice we made worth the pain?"

"Is my vengeance worth the pain it might cause? Is that the point?"

"Yes!" he said raising his hand. "But first you have to declare the worth as material or spiritual. So, which is it?"

"Both," I said.

"Nope," he said. "Can't be done together. Either can stand alone, but neither can be used with the other. Apples and oranges. So, which do you choose?"

"I can't choose," I said. "I have responsibilities in both."

His eyes burned into me. "Life is that choice. One is temporary and one is eternal."

"You've changed the subject," I said. "The question was whether justice is worth the pain it might cause, but I've yet to find pain in knowing that bad people get what they deserve. Where is the pain in that?"

He smiled. "And now you've changed the subject. But I'll go with you. Justice? Who decides what they deserve? You? Be very careful about assuming you know what people deserve. You can't even describe your love for your wife, and you can determine the needed pain for others? The pain, my new friend, is in changing the subject." He looked down at the ground as an ant crawled on his shoe and started the long journey up his pant leg. He reached down and squashed the bug between two fingers. "Poor misguided creature," he said. "Don't forget. The pain can be unbearable at times, without aspirin."

Neither of us said anything for a long time. "That ant killed himself by choosing his path up your leg. It was his decision."

He looked concerned. "That ant has no soul," he said. "That ant can't even imagine not existing."

I stood up.

"Here," he said. "Help an old man up." And he raised his hand for me to take. He was light and I raised him easily.

"Thanks for your time, Mr. Acree."

"Thanks for crossing my path," he said. "I'll walk with you any day. And you know why?"

"No sir."

"Because all I want is for you to find peace," he said. "And that means whatever pain I may find with you as my friend is worth it." He looked at me with deep blue eyes. "That should answer your question," he said, smiling like he knew all along my entire plan and he was somehow attached to some source of knowledge much bigger than me. I suddenly felt very small.

Later in the afternoon, Taylor and I were sitting on the tailgate of her truck, when John Russell and Julia arrived. His truck was loaded with clothes and guns and boxes of books and two blue heeler dogs. Jasper greeted the blue dogs with the appropriate combative posturing, until Taylor scolded him and said it was okay. Jasper's hair remained bristled, even when he came to her side and sat obediently. The blue dogs said nothing, but constantly looked to John for direction. He emerged from the truck smiling and quietly said "stay" and the dogs lay down on his coats. Julia was laughing as usual these days when she shut the door.

"We're home," she said, as she made her way directly to Taylor and hugged her neck. "We brought food."

"Ya'll need some help?" Taylor asked.

"No, ma'am," John said. "We'll get this stuff unloaded and then I'll get the animals fed and then Julia and I will fix supper."

"That would be great," Taylor said.

"My dogs won't cause a problem, Miss Taylor. I promise, but when you can, I need to introduce you so they'll know you're family...." And he stopped. "I mean, well...they're real protective."

"I signed the papers yesterday. I am your legal guardian so you can go to school here. You are family, John," I said.

He looked down and then back up. "You'll never know...." And he stopped. "I'll do you a good job. I promise."

"What are their names?" Taylor asked.

"Doc is the boy dog. Ki is the girl."

"Tell 'em why," Julia said.

"Why?"

"The reasons for the names," she said.

John looked embarrassed and then shrugged, as if arguing with Julia was a lost fight. "A doctor is a healer. So, Doc is my heeler. And Ki is short for Kiowa."

"Doc and Ki," Taylor said. "I like those names."

"Well, we better get going. We'll find you in about an hour and get cooking."

"We'll be out back," Taylor said.

And they started the truck and pulled away, leaving us watching and smiling to ourselves.

"Are they happy or what?" I said.

"They've been inseparable since day one," she said. "He took her fishing in the creek yesterday and they cooked fresh fish for me last night. They came walking back across the field, wet up to their waists, carrying two stringers of bass and bluegill and I could hear them laughing the whole way. Well, she was laughing, so I assume he was saying something."

"I'm sorry I missed that," I said.

"Me, too," she said. "Working?"

"Yeah, we had to serve some warrants last night, but it's funny, at one time all I could think about was wondering what you were doing," I said.

"You should have called," she said.

I smiled, but said nothing.

"Was it violent?" she asked.

"No. Well, kind of. Nothing to worry about," I said.

"Yeah, right," she said. And then she didn't say anything for a while. "Want a drink?" she finally asked.

"Do you do that?"

"Do what?"

"Have thoughts when we're apart," I said.

"Of violence?"

"No. Of me."

She laughed and shook her head. "You already know the answer to that," she said.

"No, I don't."

She jumped off the tailgate and stood in front of me and looked me in the eyes. "Oh, pretty much all day, every day," she said. "Now, you want the drink?"

"Absolutely," I said.

And we sat on the back porch and had drinks, watching the sun fade, and the new leaves moved in the breeze and we talked about John and Julia and blue dogs in trucks and then the kids showed up and John threw some marinated deer back strap on the grill and Julia had one glass of wine and we all sat together on the porch and ate medium rare venison and baked potatoes and salads while the sky became black and we watched for shooting stars. I said very little and I caught Taylor looking at me like something was wrong. My silence was linked to everything feeling so right, but there were no words to surround the feeling. So I just smiled. And finally, she just smiled back, like she knew.

CHAPTER 18

The next day I caught two boys hunting turkeys over bait and issued them citations. They were real nice and seemed truly surprised that I was anywhere around, not knowing their neighbor had called the previous day and reported the bait because one of them owed him ten dollars.

I checked back at Hank's Store around one, but Tiller was a no show. W.B. called on his way back to Humphreys County and checked on John Russell. He seemed happy that John was settled and finding new country to explore. A normal day.

I made a pass through the southeastern part of the county, where I had spent little time and tried to get a lay of the roads. I arrived back at the cabin about five and had just let Berit out to run when my phone rang.

"Mr. Stewart. This is John. You better come up here. Miss Taylor needs you and she won't let us help," he said calmly.

"Talk to me, John," I said. "What's going on?"

"No bad guys," he said. "She's not hurt. Just crying. She's by the barn."

When I got close, I could see her truck parked by the barn and she was sitting on the ground at the rear tire. Jasper was in her lap and she held him with both arms rocking back and forth. I walked toward her. There was blood on her shirt and arms and her face was buried in his side as she rocked. I could hear her sobbing. She looked up as I neared her.

"I didn't know he was under the truck," she cried. "Why didn't he move?"

I sat next to her and leaned my back against the truck. Our shoulders touched and I moved my hand across Jasper's head and across his neck to her hand and I took it.

She squeezed my hand and cried again and I noticed the dog's blood around her fingernails and in her hair as she held the dog closer as she rocked again.

I said nothing.

She looked up. "I got in the truck and looked and didn't see anything, so I backed up to turn around, felt a bump, and I looked in the mirror and his legs were sticking out. I jumped out and pulled him out and he was dead." She looked directly at me. "Why, Ethan? Why didn't he move?"

I shook my head. I whispered. "I'm so sorry, Taylor. I know how you loved him. You took great care of him. He was your dog. And when something like this happens, you want to know why, but there is no why. These things just happen sometimes and you just get through it."

"How? It's so senseless! There is no reason for this. It teaches no lesson. There is no good that could come of this. It just hurts," she said.

I released her hand and put my arm around her shoulder, and she turned to put her head on my chest so that she, the dog and me became one. And I held her for a long time and stroked her hair while she cried.

"I can't leave him for a while," she whispered.

"I'm not going anywhere," I whispered back. "We'll sit here all night, if you want. Just cry. Go ahead and just cry, cause the dog deserves all the tears you've got. Cause he was a good dog."

"He was," she said.

I whispered some more. "I had this dog when I was a young game warden, named Dusky. He was a black Lab and we rode together every day for seven years. He was my best friend. We worked together and hunted together and he was friends to my children and wife. He had total run of the house and was a true gentleman of a dog. Never misbehaved and the most loyal friend I ever had. One day Dusky was feeling bad, you know, didn't have the normal energy, so I thought he was just under the weather and I left him home to rest. When I got home, he was laying by the side of the house and when I got close to him, he started convulsing and he died in my arms while I sat in the grass. One day he was fine and the next he was dead. I cried for seven days. Sometimes, after three or four days, I thought I had it beat and I would be driving down the road and think of him gone and cry some more."

"I've lost dogs before," she said. "But it never hurt like this."

"I know," I said. "It's okay. The only thing I can tell you is it's gonna hurt for a while and I won't leave you, unless you want me to, as long as it lasts."

And she grabbed my hand and squeezed hard. "Please don't leave," she said.

"I won't, Taylor. I won't leave you." And we sat there for a long time until the sun started sinking and she would cry and then be still and then cry some more, the entire time holding the bloody dog that used to be her friend.

John and Julia approached at dusk and stood in front of us. They said nothing and Julia was softly crying.

"Ya'll have a seat," I said. "We're just gonna stay here and cry for a while longer."

Julia sat next to her cousin who was more like a sister and then she cried on Taylor's shoulder until Taylor was helping her and John just stood there, watching.

"Sit down, John," I said. "You might as well get used to this cause your new family obviously cries a lot at the loss of a good dog."

And John sat across from the dog and his lip trembled and he spoke to the ground when he said, "And that's why I love my new family."

Julia looked up and saw him teary and moved to him and held him and he held her, and I couldn't tell if he was crying over the dog, or his mother, or the fact that we all were mourning.

'Okay," I said. "Here's what we're gonna do. John, go get some wood and build us a small fire. Julia, go get some blankets and pillows and sleeping bags, if you can find some. We're gonna stay out here all night, if Taylor wants to and have us a wake for a good dog who lived a great life with a woman who loved him. And that's all a good dog can ask for." I looked at Taylor. And her lips were trembling again.

"I love you guys," she whispered.

We said nothing.

"Ethan, would you and John please bury him? I can't...." And she cried again.

"Sure," I said. "Where?"

"Behind the house, overlooking the bottom," she said. "But we'll be here cause I can't go in the house tonight."

John immediately got up and went to the barn, returning with a shovel and I took the dog from her lap and she hugged him one more time and then looked away.

When we settled on the gravesite, I laid Jasper on the ground, as John began digging. I searched the dog's left side carefully, parting the hair around the blood.

John stopped. "What are you looking for?"

"Bullet hole," I said.

"You think...?"

"I don't know," I said.

"I didn't hear a shot," he said leaning on the shovel.

"You might not've been able to if they have a suppressed weapon," I said.

"Who?" he asked.

"I tell you later, but you keep your eyes open around here." And I turned the dog over, searching the right side.

"Have you got a pistol?"

"Yes, sir."

"What kind?"

"Colt 1911," he said.

"Can you shoot it?"

"Yes sir."

"I mean, are you good?

"Very," he said.

"Who taught you?"

"W.B."

"Enough said," I said. "Start carrying it around here."

"Won't that scare the girls?" he asked.

"Conceal it, if you want, but wear it."

"I can't take it to school," he said while digging.

"Not inside the building, but you can have it in your truck. Just hide it," I said.

"I could get in trouble," he said.

"You sure could," I said. "If you need it and don't have it…that's trouble. Don't worry about school. I'll handle it. This ain't Nashville you know. We're kinda in the heartland of America out here."

"Yes sir. I'll take care of it," he said.

"Don't let anyone hurt them when I'm not here," I said. "Whatever you have to do. Do it."

He stopped digging and threw the shovel on the ground. "No one will hurt them while I'm alive. I promise you that," he said with a voice much older than his years. "Find anything?"

"No bullet holes," I said. "But if I find out they did this to her dog, I'll kill all of them."

"All of who?" he asked.

"The Mabrys," I said. "Watch out for a big guy named Spike. He has a thing for Julia. He's big and slow, but if he gets his hands on you, it could be bad. I'll take care of the others."

"Yes sir, but you need to know that Julia will be fine. Don't worry about her. Concentrate on the others, cause nothing will happen to Julia."

I smiled at him. "You kinda like that girl, huh?"

And for the first time, John smiled back at me. "There ain't no words," he said.

And we gently placed the dog in the grave and I smoothed his hair and said, "You're a good dog, Jasper," before finishing the job.

When we returned to the truck, the girls had already built a small fire and the blankets were laid out around the fire. They had brought wine and whiskey and food and they were one drink ahead of us. I looked up and the sky was clear with shining stars and there was no wind. The smoke from the fire went straight up and the wood crackled in its early life.

Taylor poured me a whiskey over ice and Julia offered the wine bottle to John.

"No," he said. "I want what they're drinking, but understand it's only a toast to Jasper." Julia smiled and poured him a shot over ice. John sat at the fire and tasted the whiskey. He made a face. "You guys actually like that?"

"It's an acquired taste," I said.

He took another sip. "If you say so," he said. "Miss Taylor, would you mind if I called my dogs. They might be lonely in a new place."

She smiled and I noticed her eyes were swollen in the firelight. "Please call your dogs," she said. "Where are they?"

"In the back of my truck," he said. He stood and whistled once and two blue streaks came running around the barn and didn't stop until at John's feet, where they looked up at him and then lay down. John sat at the fire and the dogs moved closer, touching him.

"They're trained well," she said.

"I think they're just real smart," he said.

"Would they come to me if I called?" she asked.

"Ki would," he said.

She reached her hand toward the dogs. "Come here, Ki," she said softly, and the dog looked at her and then back at John.

"It's okay," he said. And the blue dog stood and very slowly walked around the fire to Taylor, smelling her hand, and she touched its head and slowly stroked behind its ears and the dog shut its eyes, moving its head into her fingers. "What is it about good dogs?" she said.

"The loyalty is the thing," I said. "A good dog is the best of all the good friends, lovers, and family rolled into one bag of fur and bones. But the loyalty is thing that makes us cry."

John and Julia were petting Doc at the fire's edge. "My mom said that we should all take lessons from dogs," he said. "She said that a good dog only has one focus and that's pleasing its master. She said if we were that focused, our lives would be complete."

"What master?" Julia asked.

And John looked at her. "God," he said. "She believed that if we were that focused and loved God that much that He would take care of everything and give us peace."

"That's a hard thing to do," I said. "Stay focused on goodness."

"I know," he said. "I'm stuck between a mother who was an angel and a father who died fighting to protect us. I love them both. And I'm not sure how to be true to both of them."

The fire popped, sending sparks skyward. "I wonder what that's like?" Julia said. "To have parents you love and respect. My father's a drunk and hits my mom. My mother's so shallow and mean, she probably deserves it."

I thought about that. "Some say we shouldn't judge what people deserve," I said. "But it's a hard thing not to do."

John took another drink and made another face. Julia laughed at him. "I think this stuff gets worse," he said.

I looked at Taylor to see if she was laughing, but she had lain down on the blanket and the blue heeler was curled in front of her as she stroked its side. "I like your dog," she said out loud. "Thank you, John." And I saw her head trembling as she silently cried, holding her new friend named Ki.

Later, when the coals were only glowing and no one had spoken for a long time and John and Julia were lying under their blankets staring at the fire, Taylor spoke again. "I want to know her name," she said.

"Who?" I said.

Taylor sat up with the dog in her lap and she turned to face me. "Your wife. I want you to tell me about her."

I didn't say anything for a while, but stared into the coals, a thousand mental pictures of Jenny flooding my memory. A thousand conversations...

"I've got all night," Taylor said.

I poured another drink and took a sip, the whiskey burning my throat or maybe it was something else that caused the burning. I'm not sure.

"Jenny. Her name was Jenny. And I never called her Jen or Jennifer. It was Jenny. She was five-feet, five, brown hair that streaked naturally in the summer. Brown eyes. Beautiful eyes. Delicate small wrists and ankles.

Very smart. Loved animals, sunrises and sunsets. Laughed a lot. Always positive. Great swimmer. She swam across the lake and back every day in the summer. When she drank too much, which was rare, she would touch her nose, because she said that was the first sign of too much, a numb nose. And then she would get sleepy."

I looked across the coals and saw John touch his nose and we all laughed.

"I think I'm okay," he said.

"Her favorite song was 'To the Morning' by Dan Fogelberg. Her favorite movie was *Dances with Wolves*. And both made her cry. She is the best friend I've ever had and I miss her every day. She was the finest person I've ever known, and until I came here and met you all, that's all I had...missing her."

"How did she die?" she asked.

I took another long drink. "Aneurism in the brain. They say it's instant death. But she was swimming, maybe a hundred yards from our dock and I was watching. She was there and then she wasn't. I remember waiting for her to reappear. And after a few seconds, she didn't, so I jumped in the boat and went out there and I dove in, but I couldn't be sure where she had been. I dove and dove and every time I would come up I would pray that she was there and just joking with me." And I stopped talking.

Taylor was crying again. Julia was crying. John was staring at me with eyes that understood. And I took a deep breath and finished. "I couldn't find her."

"I'm sorry," Taylor whispered.

"Like you said, seems so senseless," I said.

A coyote cried in the distance and another joined in and they sang for thirty seconds and then it was quiet again.

"My mom said a nursing baby has no sense of motherhood and can't explain it, and we are the same throughout our lives," John said. "We should just have faith that we are being cared for."

And those words were the last I remember of that night.

In the morning, when the first light of day warmed our faces and the coals were black and dew covered and a strong smell of hickory hung around us, I opened my eyes. My arm was around Taylor and the dog named Ki and there was warmth between us under that blanket. John and Julia were cuddled on the other side of the fire, sleeping peacefully. It was a new day. And we were somehow stronger than the day before.

CHAPTER 19

I was reluctant to leave Taylor, but she said she had to stop crying and because I made it so comfortable for her to cry and grieve, she wouldn't quit if I stayed. At ten, she called and said I should have stayed because she hadn't quit crying since Julia and John and I left. I wanted to go home and be with her, but I didn't.

I forced myself to think of Tiller Mabry. I was confused as to how this man could attract so many people around him. He was charismatic, in a sick, demonic sense, but that attribute, in itself, would not explain the people around him. It had to be money.

The big money that could be attached to Houston County was not drugs, or illegal deer meat, or guns, Tiller's past activities. The mussel industry had collapsed when the Japanese quit paying big bucks for Kentucky Lake mussel shells. It had to be caviar.

In 1982, when Ronald Reagan imposed an embargo on Iran because of the hostage situation, it started the demise of the world's market on Beluga caviar. And then when the Soviet Union collapsed, so did the controls on Caspian Sea sturgeon, the natural producer of the world's supply of high priced caviar. Within ten years, the fish was nearly gone, and so went the eggs. The closest substitute was found in great numbers in Kentucky Lake...the Tennessee River paddle fish. The roe produced by Tennessee paddle fish was not quite the same taste, but very close, and for those who were not caviar experts, easily confused. The Russians then began a buying frenzy of Tennessee fish and even marketed the paddle fish caviar as Caspian Sea Sturgeon caviar, at inflated prices. And suddenly, some Tennessee commercial fishermen who made modest livings catching buffalo and catfish became infatuated with the possibilities of making big money by shifting to paddle fish and harvesting the eggs. We had seen a disturbing number of paddle fish dead, with their bellies ripped open by untrained fishermen who could catch the fish, but killed male and female fish, looking for eggs. And then we found the real problem.

The Russian mafia found that backwoods fishermen were reluctant to do business with strange foreigners with Yankee license plates, and so they made contacts with locals who could do the egg buying and then buy from them. It was actually cheaper that way, for the locals could cut a better deal in the buying process, and even though they may skim a bit, the profits were much larger. Enter Tiller Mabry. But after Samuel's murder and the trial, the Russians disappeared and all our covert intelligence dried up.

I met Sam, the braid, at ten-thirty in a little town named Van Leer, just back from the mountains and his bear buy. We figured it to be far enough away from Houston County to be safe, and who would go to a place named Van Leer unless you lived there. We sat in the parking lot of the Co-op and drank thermos coffee.

"What have I missed?" he said.

"Not much. One more conversation with Tiller. Tom'll let you listen. He says he's gonna kill me."

"I would be careful, Chief," he said.

"Why?"

"You mean besides he's a psychopath, it appears his connections with the Russians were pretty deep. It seems he convinced them that he could control the entire Kentucky Lake roe harvest and control the legal system to protect the Russians' interest," he said.

"How do you know? I mean what's happened different than what we knew just before Samuel was killed?" I said.

"When we documented Tiller's meet with that lawyer in Nashville, we started looking at higher levels. The Service had ties in New York that led them to an Iranian banker, who had connection with a New York lawyer who has been talking a lot lately with our lawyer in Nashville. They cross-checked money transfers from the Iranian and a large sum of money was sent to New York and then Nashville to our guy who met with Tiller."

"How much money?" I asked.

"Seven hundred and fifty-thousand dollars," he said.

"I thought you said it was the Russians?" I said.

"It is. The Iranian jumped sides. He handled the legal marketing of Iranian caviar when there was legal Iranian caviar, but lately, the only game in town is with the

Russian mafia, who claim ownership of Kentucky Lake eggs, so he supplies the money and takes a hit on the take, to keep Russian banks clean."

"So how did we find out?"

"You won't believe it, but it had nothing to do with caviar. The banker is also into gun running for terrorists in Iraq. The Feds found it looking for guns. They just passed it along."

"So, your theory is that Tiller may be the front man for all the egg buying on Kentucky Lake for the Russian mafia, with money supplied by Iran?"

"In a nut shell, yes. It's a theory," he said.

"Well, that's just great," I said. "Tiller Mabry would kill a man for five hundred dollars. And now he may be in control of three quarters of a million dollars. That's just great."

Sam got out of the truck and mockingly saluted. "Just keeping you in the loop, Chief," he said. "Since you seem to be Tiller's favorite game warden and all. Watch your back, Ethan," he said.

"Where are you going?" I said.

"I'm going to meet Tom. We're gonna stick close to him for awhile. When's the next meet with him?"

"Friday week. At his house," I said. "He ought to love me coming to his house."

"Like I said, be careful," he said. And he shut my door, started his car, and left the Co-op, heading west toward Houston County.

Taylor was standing at her sink washing dishes. Julia was cooking something that smelled fabulous at the stove. They both looked up as I entered the room.

"Hey," Taylor said. "Want a drink?"

"Absolutely," I said.

And she moved to the bar and I heard ice in a glass. "How was your day?"

"Fine," I said. "Yours?"

"Cried all day," she said. "But I'm good," she said. "You said it would last about seven days. So at least I see an end to it."

"It gets easier every day," I said as she handed me the glass. "Where's John?"

"He's feeding," Julia said. "Be here in about thirty minutes for supper."

"I need to talk to him," I said. "We'll be back." I started out and then turned to Taylor. "You okay?"

She smiled at me, walked across the room, stretched up on her tip toes and kissed me on the cheek. "I'm good," she said. "Go."

I smiled back at her. "Thanks," I said. "I needed that." And I left the room smiling.

I looked in the barn, but John wasn't there, so I walked around the barn to the small house out back. I heard the guitar before I saw him on the front porch and I stopped. He was playing something melodious and I could hear his voice singing along, but I couldn't distinguish the words. He was finger picking, not strumming, and the notes were clear and purposeful. I listened for a second before approaching him. He stopped playing immediately upon hearing my footfalls and laid the guitar against the wall. The blue heelers laying at his feet looked at me and he whispered, "It's okay," and they calmed.

"I didn't know you played guitar," I said climbing the steps.

"Yeah," he said. "My mom taught me. She was real good."

"So are you," I said.

"You play?" he said.

"No, but I value a good guitar player. Always liked it."

"Ever try?"

"Little old for trying new things," I said.

"No you're not," he said. "I'll teach you."

I pulled up a chair. "Interesting thought," I said. "You know, nothing's impossible. In a cloudless sky, there's still a chance of rain."

"Since I know you better now, there's probably some deep meaning to that," he said.

I smiled across the porch at him. "Not really. Just a fact of nature that always makes me feel better."

He picked up the guitar and softly picked some notes. "My mom could come up with the best melodies. She said that God would hum tunes to her when she was the happiest."

"I wish I could've met your mother," I said.

"Yeah," he said. "She was like some force of nature. Does that make sense?"

I paused before answering. "More than you know," I said.

He stopped playing and rested his chin on the guitar body. "Can I ask you a question?"

"Sure," I said. "Shoot."

"I'm confused," he said. And he struggled to continue. "Uh, you really loved your wife, right?"

"Loved?" I said. "Used to think that word could cover it, but I'm not sure anymore. I'm not sure "love" is strong enough."

"Then what?"

"I'm not sure there are words strong enough," I said.

"How did you know? I mean in the beginning?" he said.

I took a drink and swallowed. "When I was your age, I wondered if there could be any girl who I loved who would take my arm and walk down the road with me. You know, no matter what, she would be there and love me, in spite of my weaknesses. And in the end be happy she chose me."

"And you found her?"

"I did."

"Jenny?"

"Jenny."

"Did you know from the beginning?"

"After our first real conversation, which happened pretty fast," I said.

"And you knew?"

"Absolutely."

"How?"

I paused. "The thought of us apart made me sick inside," I said.

"I know what you mean," he said.

"Do you?"

"Yep."

"Hurts real bad, huh?"

"It's awful," he said.

"In the end," I said. "It's a blessing."

He looked confused. "How can pain be a blessing?"

I smiled. "Cause she was worth the pain. And more."

He thought about that for awhile. "But how did you know she felt the same?"

"That's a tough one," I said. "She had a talent for fixing me. And one day I just knew she couldn't do that if we weren't together. You know, feeling the same."

"Fixing you?" he said.

"You know. You're bothered about something. You may not even know what it is, but something's just not right. And she knows. And she knows how to fix it, sometimes without even talking about it."

He laid the guitar against the wall again. "I told Julia I had nothing. No money. No family. No bright future."

"What did she say?" I said.

He smiled. "She said she didn't care. She said she didn't need a lot of money to be happy. She said she needed something else."

"And what was that?" I asked.

"She just smiled when I asked," he said. "She asked me if I knew when she was happy. And I said I thought so. And she said how do you know? And I said cause you can't hide happy. And she asked if I thought she was happy when we were together. And I said, yes. And she said I am and that's all you ever need to remember."

"Wow," I said.

"What's 'wow' mean?" he said.

"You might want to hold on to this girl," I said.

"Really," he said smiling.

"Really," I said. "Like I said, she fixed you."

And then John was enthusiastic. "She's like this big…uh…I don't know the word. One minute I'm thinking like she's the best friend I've ever had. I mean we talk about everything. And then I notice we've been talking an hour and it seems like three minutes and then we talk another two hours and then it seems like we just started. And then five minutes later, she's not my best friend anymore. It's a feeling that makes me feel weak and the thought of not being with her makes me hurt real deep in a place I can't describe, kinda like what you said."

I didn't say anything for a while and he finally looked up at me. "Contradiction," I said.

"Sir?"

"The word you wanted is contradiction," I said. "Your feelings for her go between best friend and lover. Right?"

He looked embarrassed. "I've never even said the word lover," he said. "I think she may just be like a girlfriend."

"I got news for you, John. The woman who gave you the unique compliment of saying your presence was all that she needed to be happy, may be your best friend, but she is much rarer than a girlfriend."

"How rare is that?"

"What? To find the perfect one? Jenny and I used to talk about that. Damn rare, I'd say. And if it happens, you ought to feel blessed."

"Kinda like that chance of rain when there aren't any clouds," he said.

"There's always the chance," I said. "So, what do you like about her?"

"I'm not sure where to start," he said. "She cares about things. I mean really cares. Like every time we see a stray dog or cat on the road, she makes me stop and we pick it up. We've brought three kittens to the barn since I've been here and Miss Taylor keeps saying that cats must find our barn, but she doesn't know that Julia and I are bringing them here. And we've picked up two pups and she's already found homes for them at school." He smiled. "I like that," he said. "And the other night she took some whiskey from the bar and came out here with a CD player and she had two drinks and, please don't be mad and tell Miss Taylor, but she danced all over this porch and kept trying to get me to dance, but I don't dance, and she didn't care, but she is so fun to be around. I've never been around anybody who made me so happy…ever, ever," he said.

"Wow," I said again.

"I'm sorry," he said. "Maybe I shouldn't have said all that."

"Why not?" I said. "If your father was here, you'd be having this conversation with him."

"You think?" he said.

"Guarantee it," I said.

"I couldn't have this talk with W.B.," he said. "I tried once."

"Doesn't mean he doesn't care," I said. "He's just not real gabby."

"Yeah," he said. "What about you and Miss Taylor?"

"What about us?"

"Julia wanted me to ask you," he said. "She said that when she asks Miss Taylor about y'all, she won't say anything. Says she just smiles."

I thought about that. "Well, like you said. You can't hide happy, can you?" I said.

He smiled. "No sir."

"Let's eat. The girls are waiting."

"Okay, but I have one more question. Why'd you come out here?" he said. "I mean, you've never come out here before."

"Had something to tell you, but it'll keep," I said. "I'm not adding anything to this conversation." And we walked down the steps of that porch and headed toward the house where Taylor and Julia were waiting and I wondered what conversations they had in our absence.

"I have another question," I said as we walked.

"Okay."

"Does Julia like Jimmy Buffet?"

"Who's he?"

"Jimmy Buffet," I said. "You know the singer?"

"Oh, yeah. He's the guy who sings about beaches and rum."

"Yeah. That's him."

"Don't remember ever hearing her mention him. But she does talk about if we won the lottery...I mean if she won the lottery, she wanted to buy an island and walk beaches."

"Hmm," I said. "And what do you say about that?"

"Well," he said. "I reckon I'd have to learn how to catch salt-water fish to stay real happy, but I'll tell you Mr. Stewart, if she won the lottery and asked me to go with her, I'd be heading south."

I laughed out loud. "It's Ethan, John. Enough of this, Mr. Stewart stuff."

"Okay," he said. "Wonder what they fixed for supper?"

"Not sure. I really don't care. Just glad we have a place to end the day with two women that make us happy," I said.

"Amen to that," he said. "Does that mean you like her?"

"Amen to that," I said. "And then some."

We took a few steps without talking. "You wearing the Colt?"

"Yes sir. Said I would. I always do what I say," he said.

"Good. I appreciate it. Makes me feel better, and you need to know. I trust very few people in this world. I trust you."

"You can," he said. "And I'm as loyal as the best dog you ever rode with."

I took a few steps. "Wow," I whispered to myself for the third time in one conversation.

CHAPTER 20

The next night we double dated, but John and Julia sat at a separate table. I thought separate tables a smart thing because they needed the privacy, or maybe I was feeling the same. We tried Mary's Restaurant at Taylor's suggestion. Home cooked buffet and salad bar with Tennessee River catfish as the entrée. I asked the waitress to bring me John's ticket and she said sure thing honey. After getting John and Julia's drink order, she came back to us and said, "Are those two kids in love or what?"

"Could be," she smiled.

"Oh, I remember the days," the waitress said and smiled all the way back to the kitchen.

"Okay," Taylor said. "You're so observant, what is it that makes people know when two people are in love? What did she see?"

I turned and looked at John and Julia. They didn't see me turn. They didn't see anybody else in the room. They didn't see the plates in front of them. They didn't see the room around them. They didn't know they were on planet Earth. "Aliens," I said. "She saw people from another planet where nothing matters except the other alien in front of them."

She took a bite of salad, like she was not interested in the food. "Does that look go away with age?"

"What look?"

"The 'obviously in love' look," she said.

"No," I said. "We just get better at hiding it."

"Why?"

"Cause we've been hurt," I said. "We avoid vulnerability."

"You said you're vulnerable with me," she said.

"I did. And I also said it scared the hell out of me."

She paused and stabbed a tomato wedge. "You've got a mean streak," she said. "Where'd that come from?"

"Mean? Not a mean bone in my body," I said.

"Then how come people are scared of you?" she said.

"Are they?"

"Yep."

"Who?"

"Pretty much anyone who doesn't know you," she said.

"Not true," I said. "Little ol' ladies love me."

She smiled and ate another bite. "You could probably leave off the 'little old' part."

"Not true again," I said. "Some women don't like me at all."

"Name some," she said.

"The ones I really don't like," I said. "Can't seem to hide my feelings."

"Imagine that," she said.

"You think I'm mean?" I said.

"I think you're extremely firm," she said. "But don't change the subject. Describe a woman you don't like?"

I thought about that. "A woman who doesn't care about important things. They generally insult me by thinking I buy into their lack of values."

"Define important things," she said.

"I'd rather define unimportant things," I said taking a bite of fish. "Like money or vanity or country clubs or power by association."

"I like money," she said.

"So do I," I said. "But you've never used money to try to impress me."

"Who says I want to impress you?" she said.

"I don't think you do," I said. "That's one thing I really like about you. I think you're pretty much take me or not."

"We are all vain to a point," she said. "I may have had my nose fixed," she said. "How do you think I feel now?"

"Glad you didn't," I said.

She smiled again. "You don't know," she said. "I may have a great plastic surgeon."

"You do," I said. "God."

She laughed. "Well, what could I do to impress you, I mean, if I wanted to try?"

"Maybe you already have," I said.

"Maybe?"

"Okay, you have, but we're still learning."

"Is that what we're doing?" she said.

"Yes, ma'am."

"What have you learned?"

"Lots."

"Okay, what's still to learn?"

"Lots."

She placed her fork on the table and smiled, like she was just before throwing something at me. "Name one thing you need to learn. And answer the damn question."

"Technically, that wasn't a question." And before she could say anything, I answered the damn question. "Why your tone of voice changes on the phone."

She looked surprised. "Explain."

"We talk on the phone during the week and you're the same. Even when your mood changes, you are the same girl. Not so on the weekends. You can be detached. Sometimes our conversations are forced."

"You're crazy," she said.

"It's true. And I don't understand it," I said.

"Maybe it's because of you," she said. "You work every weekend and you may be in that work tone."

"It's still me," I said. "Working or not."

"It's still me," she said. "Weekend or not."

"Nope. It's a different girl."

"You know what?" she said.

"What?"

"You think too much," she said.

"Really?"

"Yes," she said. And she picked up her fork and ate with enthusiasm.

"You know what?" I said.

"What?" she said chewing.

"Whenever you say, 'You know what', you're mad about something."

She smiled. "You know me pretty good."

"Fast learner," I said. "And something else, you've got a mean streak of your own."

"Do not," she said. "Just firm, like you."

"Hmmm," I said.

"And no cosmetic surgery, either…anywhere," she said.

"I wasn't even going there," I said.

"I've noticed," she said while chewing.

"Ouch," I said. "You are mean."

"No, I'm not. But I am very patient."

"I like patient," I said. "Sometimes I think we're so much alike, it's scary."

"I wonder if that's a good thing?" she said.

"Well, I've never believed that opposites attract and last."

"I agree," she said. "But we are different, you and me."

"How?"

"I don't over-think things," she said.

I laughed. "Oh really? You think a lot, but you're real stingy about letting your thoughts out."

She looked at me. "Maybe safer that way," she said.

"It's just me," I said. "Let 'em out."

"Let 'em out and sometimes you can't get them back."

"When I let my deep thoughts out, I don't want them back. They're a gift."

"You owe me, by the way," she said.

"Owe you what?" I said.

"You owe me a reading. Remember?"

"Ah," I said. "I do. When?"

"Soon," she said. "I like your voice. How's that for letting a private thought out?"

"You want it back?" I said.

"Nope," she said. "It's all yours."

"Thanks," I said. "And the world didn't stop turning on its axis. Your heart's still beating and everything."

She just looked at me. "Sometimes, you just need to be quiet," she said.

"I can't read to you if I'm quiet," I whispered.

"You know what?" she said.

"I do. I'll shut up now," I said.

She just smiled.

Later, after dessert and coffee, Julia and John came to our table, but they didn't sit. I looked up at them.

"The waitress said you had our check," John said.

"I do," I said.

"I would have paid for our meal," he said.

"I know," I said. "But I'm old and I wanted to buy y'all's supper. Is that okay?"

"Yeah, and you're still way cool for an old guy," Julia said and she slapped me on the back. "Isn't he, Taylor?"

"I don't know," Taylor said. "I'm still learning. He may be way cool. I'm not sure."

"Well, thanks for supper," John said. "We're going out to the truck and listen to some music. Y'all take your time."

"We're almost through," I said. "Be right out." And they turned and left and we watched them through the window walk across the parking lot to Taylor's truck. They were holding little fingers as they walked.

"Fine looking couple, don't you think?" I said.

Taylor looked proud. "They're good kids."

"You know he plays guitar?" I said.

"Yeah, I heard him one night after Julia took some Knob Creek and snuck off to his porch," she said.

"You know about that?" I said.

"You know about that?" she said.

We smiled at each other. "You haven't told me about your daughters," she said.

"Two girls raised exactly the same with the same values. One, the younger, Abby, is a doctor in Rhode Island. Married and happy and full of life and adventure and my true friend. Lizzy, the older, is the sweetest child I've ever known, the best with animals, and struggles every day to make sense of life. I love them both very much."

"Do they get along?"

"Strangely, yes. They are family and family is strong with us. They don't agree on much, but they love each other."

"Tell me a story about Lizzy that made you proud of her," she said.

"That's easy," I said. "When they were in high school, Abby's boyfriend broke up with her and Liz saw her crying. When Lizzy found out why, she went looking for the guy and when she found him, she decked him. Laid him on the ground and said, if you ever hurt my sister again, I'll be back."

And suddenly there was commotion at the window as customers moved to see out the window and I instantly knew something was wrong, because my gut twisted for no reason and my heart rate doubled in one second. I looked, but couldn't see because the window was crowded and Julia came running through the front door and yelled "Ethan, come quick," and then ran back out.

When I cleared the front door, I could see John standing with his back to the truck and four men around him. A fifth man was on the ground screaming, holding his leg. John looked confident. He caught my eye as I neared and held up his hand.

"It's okay," he said. "Go back inside. I got this."

And I looked at John in disbelief, trying to decipher his words, contemplating his confidence to take on five men, and his desire for me to stay away.

Julia stood next to me. I heard one man cussing John and begging him to come forward. The man on the ground was squirming in the gravel, holding his leg.

"Quick, Julia, what happened?" I said.

"They were waiting at the truck in the dark and one man tried to hit John in the back with a stick or something and John…it was so fast, I couldn't even see it. He pushed me away and said don't let Ethan come out here."

"Why?"

"I don't know, but one of them said something about Jasper."

Taylor overheard Julia's words and before I could stop her, was running toward the men. I caught her in three steps and spun her around.

"No," I said. "Julia, get her inside. Call the Sheriff and call an ambulance." Taylor fought me. "Listen to me," I said. "You need to leave." She looked at me and nodded.

But I was too late. The fight had already begun. The biggest man moved toward John with his fists up, and the other three were circling. I walked toward them but it was over before I took five steps.

I saw the big man jab once and John moved his head away from the punch and without any telegraphing of his attack, John kicked the man's knee hard, rolled once on the ground, stood and punched another in the throat before the man could even attempt a block. John faced the third man as the man swung, but John parried the punch, grabbed the man's wrist, put it in a wrist lock and drove the man's head into the bed of the pickup and turned to face the fourth man who was now backing up with his hands outstretched in front of him.

"Wait, man. Wait!" he yelled.

John grabbed the man's fingers and bent them backwards, forcing the man to his knees. The other four were on the ground. Two of them were not moving. Two of them holding their knees. I looked around and the parking lot was full of people from the restaurant, all looking with amazement at John.

I searched the men on the ground and found no guns. Then I walked to John and knelt to look in the man's eyes, while John held him.

"Don't do it, Ethan," John said.

"Tell me now about the dog," I whispered. "Tell me now, or I'll kill you." And I pulled the .45 from under my coat and snapped the safety off. It clicked. He looked down and swallowed.

"Don't know nothin' about the dog," he whispered. "I swear, I don't. Spike Mabry paid us a hundred dollars a piece to beat the shit out of this boy where people could see. He said to mention the dog. That's all I know, Buddy."

"I'm not your damn buddy. Now, when the sheriff gets here, you tell him what you just told me and you tell him that John was just protecting himself. You got it?"

"I got it," he said.

"Now, why five of you?"

"Spike said you might be with him. Four of us were for you. He's scared of you," the man said. And then his eyes turned to John. "Who are you?" he asked. And John squeezed harder and the man grimaced in pain.

John whispered. "My father's son."

"Stand him up, John." John did. I searched the man and removed his wallet. I then collected all the others' identification, about the time I heard the siren in the distance.

"Where's your gun?" I asked John.

"Small of my back," he said. I lifted his shirt and removed the Colt, and hid it in the truck as the ambulance pulled up beside us.

"Glad you didn't box them," I said.

"Wasn't much in a boxing mood," he said.

"Glad you weren't in a shooting mood," I said.

"Glad you weren't in a killing mood," he said. And that was all he said until we got home.

CHAPTER 21

Later, we sat around Taylor's kitchen table. Julia doctored John's wound where the Colt dug into his back when he rolled on the ground, causing a deep cut. Taylor was quiet.

"Quit moving," Julia said.

"What are you doing back there?" John said.

"I have to clean it," she said. "Be still."

"What's happening, Ethan?" Taylor said.

"I'll fix it," I said. "Just everybody be real careful for awhile. But I'll fix it."

"How can you fix this?" Taylor said. "You can't fix bad people."

"Yes, I can."

"How?"

"Just be careful for awhile," I said. "While John and Julia are at school, you stay close to a gun. Put the 870 in your truck. You have a pistol?"

"Yes," she said.

"What is it?"

"A revolver?"

"Short barrel or long barrel?"

"Short," she said. "A thirty eight."

"Can you shoot it?"

"If he's close enough," she said.

"That's all a pistol is for," I said. "Close stuff."

My phone rang. I checked the number. It was W.B., so I moved to the porch and left them inside.

"You called?"

"This thing is getting real," I said. "Watch your back."

"What happened?"

"Five bad guys jumped John tonight."

"Is John alive?"

"Oh, yeah."

"Then I'd say some of them are screwed up," he said.

"All of them."

"You see it?"

"It was over before I could get there and I wasn't fifty yards away," I said.

"He's well trained," he said.

"The best I've ever seen," I said. "Who taught him?"

"Friend of mine named Frank Finney and I taught him how to fight. The number one tactical instructor for our team. Frank is the most dangerous man without a gun I ever knew. He said John was the most natural talent he ever worked with."

"How does he do that? I swear, W.B., I couldn't even follow him with my eyes?"

"Smooth is fast. That's what Frank always said."

"You ever met anybody who could beat him?" I asked.

"Naw," W.B. said. "Frank maybe, but John was a lot younger then. Now, somebody'd have to shoot him. And that's where I came in. If the kid's got a gun, they're still gonna lose. And I mean pistol, rifle, or shotgun. And Ethan, when I say rifle, I mean out to a thousand yards."

"His father would be proud," I said.

"We did what we said we'd do," he said.

"I gotta go, but we're on for Friday week, unless it happens sooner," I said.

"I'll set it up," he said.

"How ya feeling?" I asked.

"Like I'm dying," he said. "So what?"

When I entered the kitchen Julia was talking and they were listening...

"...So it has to be that Spike is still mad about the pepper spray deal and now he's mad that John and me are close."

"Why wasn't Spike there?" John asked.

"Cause I told him I'd break his neck if I ever saw him around Julia again," I said. "Maybe he believed me."

"Okay, but what about Jasper?" Taylor said.

"Just talk," I said. "To start the fight."

"But how did they even know?" she said.

"Maybe I said something to a friend at school," Julia said. "Maybe it got back to him. That's all I can think of."

"One more question and don't you hide anything from me, cause I'll know if you do. John, how come you didn't want Ethan to help you?"

John looked at her and with a clear conscience said, "I knew you and Julia would be safe with Ethan and I was kind of busy. Ethan and I have a pact about you two. I didn't know if there were others."

Taylor looked at me. "Is that the truth?"

"It is," I said.

"Is that all the truth?" she said. She looked back at John.

"No," he said.

She looked at me.

"No, it's not, but it's all the truth you need to know right now."

"I don't like this," she said.

"I'm sorry, Taylor. Forgive me, but that's all I can tell you right now. Just trust me."

She looked at us for a long time. "Okay," she said.

"And if you don't mind, I need John to stay in this house for a while. You have an extra bedroom?" I said.

"Sure," she said. "What about you?"

"I'll take the couch till I'm sure things are okay, if that's all right."

"It's fine," she said.

"I know this is strange that I haven't mentioned this, but what about this Tom fellow you once mentioned. Could he show up?"

She smiled. "No. Tom and I didn't work out. He won't be coming here," she said.

I looked at her. "You sure?"

"Trust me," she said.

"Okay. I'm going to get Berit and John, get the heelers. Taylor, would you please turn your security camera back on?"

"I never turned it off," she said.

"If I was a betting man, I'd bet they won't come here," I said. "But it's better to be safe."

"Who," she asked.

"The Mabrys. Tiller and Spike and the rest."

Julia finished her bandaging and pulled John's shirt down, and kissed him on the back of the head. "Thanks," she said.

"For what?"

"Nobody's ever fought to protect me, except Taylor," she said. "I've never seen anything like what I saw tonight. Will you someday explain how you learned how to do that?"

"It's no secret," he said.

"It's almost funny. I was worried about you being the new guy at school and the bullies. No more," she said smiling.

"And after tonight," I said. "Nobody will try to fight you, John. They'll just shoot you."

"Yes sir. They may try."

"And you didn't know each other before you came here?" Taylor said to me.

"No," I said. "We didn't."

"Well, you two are very much alike," she said. "And I'm really glad you're on our side."

"We are on your side," I said. "And there's not a mean streak in either of us."

CHAPTER 22

Tuesday was Spike's court date and we climbed the steps to the court house together, the four of us. The courtroom was big and spacious, with old wooden benches, like a church. John sat with Taylor and Julia, and I moved to the officer's bench. Julia was very nervous about testifying, but held on to the courage in John's arm.

I looked around. No Spike. And when the judge entered and the bailiff said all rise, he still hadn't showed. The judge was an older, heavy set man with white hair and reading glasses. Thirty minutes later, when Spike's name was called, a man in a suit came forward with a file. He addressed the judge.

"Your honor, I represent Mr. Mabry in this case and would like to ask for a continuance as my client was stricken ill last night."

The D.A. was a short, sassy-looking blonde woman wearing a stylish business suit. "Your Honor. The state has no problem with a continuance, providing documentation can be delivered proving Mr. Mabry is indeed ill."

The lawyer looked offended. "Your Honor, my client called last night and told me he was ill. I'm here to ask for a continuance. I'm sorry if my request is suspect by the District Attorney."

The judge looked over his glasses. "Where are you from, sir?"

"Uh, Nashville, your honor."

"Your name?"

"My name is Roger Broderick, your honor."

"Mr. Broderick, describe the illness please that would not allow Mr. Mabry to come to court today."

"Well, Your Honor, he said he was sick. I didn't ask him about the illness."

"You didn't?"

"No sir. I didn't."

"So, you just figured that your client saying I'm sick was good enough to miss a court date in my court?"

"Your Honor, I didn't know a continuance would be a problem."

"This isn't a speeding ticket, Mr. Broderick. This is an assault charge on an officer. Is that how you do things in Nashville?"

I watched the D.A. She was hiding a grin, and then pretended to write something, but she wasn't writing.

"I'll find out the nature of my client's illness, Your Honor and get back with you."

The judge rubbed his eyes. "No, I'll tell you what, Mr. Broderick. I'll handle it, thanks anyway."

"Miss Jones," the judge said.

The D.A. stood. "Your Honor."

"Where is your officer?"

She turned and looked at me. I stood and approached the bench and took a position next to her. "I'm Ethan Stewart, Your Honor. I'm the arresting officer."

"Pleased to meet you, Officer Stewart. Are you that fine young wildlife officer's replacement?"

"Yes sir, I am. I am that fine young officer's replacement."

"Would you please, sir, go arrest Mr. Spike Mabry again for failure to appear, and unless he is on death's bed, have his butt back in this courtroom a week from today?"

"Yes, sir. I will."

"And Miss Jones, please see that when Mr. Mabry is arrested that he remains in custody until his court appearance."

"Yes. Your Honor. I will."

"And Mr. Broderick, are we clear on how we do things in little backwoods towns on Kentucky Lake?"

Mr. Broderick was visibly perturbed. "Yes, Your Honor. I see."

"Lower your eyes, Mr. Broderick. I don't like the way you're gazing at me," the judge said sternly.

And he did.

Miss Jones looked at me. "When can you get him?" she whispered."

"As soon as I can find him," I said. "Let's shoot for Friday at the latest."

"You know about these guys?"

"Yes ma'am," I said. "I know these guys."

"Then you know to be careful?" she said sincerely.

"Yes ma'am. I will be careful and thanks for your words."

And I turned to leave, motioning to John with my eyes to follow me out, the whole time thinking that sometimes things just fall into place perfectly.

CHAPTER 23

On Thursday night, we grilled deer meat and sweet corn. I didn't have a drink. I was not much into conversation. Taylor noticed and whispered to me after supper.

"You okay?"

"Yeah. Just thinking. I get quiet when I think too much."

"What 'cha thinkin'?"

"Work stuff," I said.

"Anything I can do to help?"

I smiled at her. "Just take care of yourself. I've kinda grown fond of you, you know."

"I do know," she said. "Me, too. So take care of yourself, will you? I'll be here when you get back," she said.

"Where am I going?" I said.

"Wherever you are tonight?" she said. "I'll be here when you get back."

"That's a good thing to know," I said.

John and Julia came to the table and sat down with bowls of vanilla ice cream. Julia placed a bowl in front of each of us. "Here," she said. "Make you sweeter."

John looked at Julia. "You need to eat two bowls, then."

"That's not nice," she said.

"I wrote a song," John said to the table.

"Really," I said. "The Lord give you a melody?"

"I believe he did," he said. "And you helped me with some words."

"When can we hear it?" Taylor said.

"I don't know," he said. "Have to get my nerve up."

"What's it about?" Julia asked.

John looked across the table. Julia was in mid-bite of a spoonful of ice cream. "You," he said. "It's about you."

She smiled with the spoon in her mouth. "Really?"

"Really," John said. And then he took his bowl to the sink, leaving Julia watching him as he walked. I looked at Taylor and she smiled back at me and the ice cream burned my throat as I swallowed the next bite.

I woke up at two a.m. with thoughts streaming. I shut my eyes, but the thoughts were relentless and no amount of concentration could stop their flowing.

I think differently about life now than ten years ago. I suppose the idea of two realities playing out at the same time was a long time coming in my mind. We are forced to deal with the reality of earthly survival from an early age. That's pure instinctual biology. Physical survival has been genetically passed down for thousands of generations. The American male culture enforces biological survival with its own identity. I call it the John Wayne philosophy. "I will not be wronged, insulted, or laid hands on," the Duke had reportedly said.

I have lived through a period of masculine transition, from the time of my father when men knew exactly what they wanted to become and the only struggle was getting there, to the present where a man chooses a course and the struggle is finding himself along the way. I hate generalities, but a portion of the truth is found there, at least in my life.

Both my parents were rooted in backwoods Tennessee, where families are inescapably held captive by trees and clear-running creeks, tobacco barns and hayfields, hounds and horseshoes, home-made whiskey and poverty. Regardless of financial standings, residents of small towns in Tennessee are faced with the poverty. There are no segregated classes. Life is collaged in its course, mixing penny loafers with over-sized hand-me-down boots, expensive silver braces with decayed blackened teeth, and store-bought Jack Daniels with basement-brewed muscadine wine. It's a wonderful blend of reality, providing everyone a glimpse of what they might become…in both directions. Me and Tiller Mabry.

I was up at four or at least that's when I finally gave up on sleep and rolled off the couch. I drank two cups of coffee on the back porch while Taylor slept in the room down the hall. Before daylight, I sneaked into her room and kissed her cheek in the darkness of the room. She smiled without opening her eyes, and I left quietly.

Friday morning was clear with no wind.

CHAPTER 24

The Mabry house stood alone at the back of Stilly Hollow with one houseless road leading to its front door. High timbered ridges surrounded the structure, and its small barn, two out buildings, and assorted vehicles in various states of repair or despair. We decided to do the confrontation in the front yard. Surveillance of the house was easy from distant ridge tops, and we could always know who occupied the house at any given time.

The video evidence of the meeting would be taken from one of the out buildings, easily accessible in the dark from the woods behind it. Sam and Tom would handle that. They would carry shotguns. Our covert unit supplied the wire for me to be audio recorded, with a direct tap into an ear phone for W.B., so he could hear everything that was being said.

W.B. chose a pastured hilltop for his bench. The bench was portable, but so heavy it took two men to assemble. They hid it in a honeysuckle patch. The sun would be at their backs at ten a.m. and the laser rangefinder showed the position to be four hundred and twenty-two yards from the front porch steps.

There was a logging road that ran from the back yard into the timber. It connected on the ridge top to another logging road that ran twelve miles through Westvaco Timber Company lands along Kentucky Lake. There were various avenues of escape off those roads, so Sam and Tom were to cover the back door from the outhouse. All these precautions were to stop the Mabrys, if by chance I was attacked or killed. Not to be melodramatic, but there was that chance and we try to be prepared for the worse.

The plan was finished. There would be no escape if they tried something stupid, but the least of their problems was the two officers in position beside the house. Their worst nightmare was the one man behind the rifle. The longest distance W.B. would have to make a shot was five hundred yards. Things weren't interesting for W.B. until the range was seven hundred yards with the .260. Five hundred yards was a chip shot.

I contacted W.B. at seven by radio. The report was that Sam and Tom had made it safely to the out building and they were set up with the surveillance gear. Luckily, there were no dogs. W.B. was in position watching the house. These men were serious, as I had seen them before numerous times in dangerous details. No jokes. No laughing. Just business.

At nine-thirty, I stopped my truck at the turn-off to the gravel road that winded a half mile to the Mabry house. I pulled the portamobile radio from under the seat and keyed the microphone.

"Thirteen twenty-one to thirteen eighteen."

"Go ahead," came W.B.'s voice in a whisper.

"I'm ready. Still go?"

"10-4."

"Anything else?" I asked.

"Two things," he said. "DO NOT block my shot. Turn off the radio. Remember, those of us watching your back will be talking while you're down there. Would not be good if they hear."

"10-4," I said. "I'm rolling." I turned the radio off.

The gravel popped under my tires on the road, and I tried to still my racing heart. Just a conversation. Done it a thousand times. Nothing to worry about. I thought about my dead young friend and his wife and children. I thought about Taylor and Julia and John. And the apprehension left immediately, replaced with anger and I quickly pushed the anger away. Anger was no good here. Anger promotes action. Anger confuses good intentions. Anger could get me killed.

The house came into view two hundred yards away. An old house, with chipped gray paint. Four windows on the front; two downstairs, two upstairs. No shades. It looked quiet. No activity in the yard. Two drivable trucks parked by the porch and a four-wheeler. Various vehicles parked in the side yard....all junkards.

I parked behind the two trucks and shut off the engine. I waited for movement in the house. There was a flash at the right window like a curtain moved and then it was still. The front door finally opened and a figure emerged from the darkness of the room. It watched for a second and then walked onto the porch. She was about twenty and wore a Budweiser T-shirt and jeans. The girl from the bar. Her hair was uncombed and tangled. Her small breasts bounced with each step, until she stopped at the porch rail looking at me.

"Whadoyouwant?" she said.

I stepped from the truck and stood facing her. "Spike around?"

"Who wants to know?" she said.

"I suspect he can see me. He knows who I am."

"He ain't here," she said. "You best leave."

"He's here, ma'am."

"You callin' me a fuckin' liar?" she said with a rising voice.

"No ma'am. How 'bout Tiller? He around?"

Tiller emerged from the door wearing an open shirt and holding a beer. He walked to the girl, whispered in her ear, and urinated off the porch, facing me. I waited.

"Morning Carp Cop," he said. "So you're lookin' for my kid brother?"

"Yeah, I need to arrest him again. Judge hated he missed court on Tuesday."

"I heard that. My dumb ass brother is inside. Why don't you come get him?"

"Let's talk," I said. "No fighting. No arguing. Just talk."

"Hey," he said taking a drink. "Where'd Samuel's wife get to. She plum disappeared after the killing. She's fuckin' hot. I need to look her up. Where is she anyway?"

"Why don't you come off the porch and talk down here," I said.

"Why don't you step away from the truck and raise yore shirt," he said.

I did. "I'm not armed, Tiller. I'm not carrying any guns. Didn't come here to do any shooting."

"Hell, that ain't smart," he said. "I'm armed." The front door opened and all Tiller's brothers stepped to the porch along with a fat short-haired man I had never seen. All except Spike. "Get on the four-wheeler and look around," Tiller commanded. "See if he brought friends."

Edward Mabry never took his eyes from me as he walked down the porch steps, cranked the ATV and headed back the way I had come.

"I gotta question," Tiller said. "All this Boy Scout shit, tryin' to protect the game and such. Is it worth dying for?"

"You gonna kill me, Tiller? That what you're saying?"

Tiller smiled and took a pull on the beer. "Anything could happen," he said. "But I'm really thinkin' about the guilt you must bare for sending that boy to the grave."

"I haven't killed anybody," I said,

"Neither did I," he said quickly.

"Yes, you did."

"Court says I didn't. I'm a free man. You don't believe in the law of the land, Stewart?"

"I believe in right and wrong," I said. "You're wrong."

"No!" he yelled. "I'm right. The court says I'm right. Who says your right is better'n the court?"

"What is right to you? What is good?"

"Damn," he said. "Ain't we getting deeper'n hell? I'll tell you what's right, Game Warden. Everything's out there for the takin'. Take care of yore family and take all you can get. That's good. That's right."

"Survival of the fittest, huh?" I said.

"Yeah, I've heard that," he said smiling.

"So you're a Darwinist?"

"Fuck Darwin, whoever the hell he is," he said.

I leaned on the truck hood. "Who taught you that about getting all you can? Your stepdad or your real daddy?"

The four wheeler drove back into the yard and Edward got off.

"Who taught you?" Tiller asked me. "Your Sunday School teacher. Your mamma? Your queer Boy Scout leader?"

"Ain't nobody with him, Tiller," Edward announced.

"You sure?" Tiller asked.

"Yeah, Tiller. Nobody's here."

"You damned sure," Tiller said again.

"Yeah."

"Then make the call." Edward motioned to the fat man, who went inside the house. There was a pause and Tiller stared at me.

"What you did was wrong, Tiller. I know what you did. We all know. We know about Slack. We know where he is."

Tiller paused again. "Old Slack's back in Detroit, I guess," Tiller said.

"No, Slack's under thirty feet of cold water in Kentucky Lake feedin' fish."

Tiller paused for the third time.

"News to me," he said.

"Do the right thing. Confess. You'll feel better," I said.

Tiller looked down at the porch and then looked up. "Okay," he said. "You've beat me down. I confess. We tied a bacon grease rag on the frame of Miss Taylor's truck when she bought feed at the Co-op. And I confess it had a drug in it and I guess it could have caused a dog to lick it and pass out under the truck. Which could make her run over her own dog." He looked at me and smiled. "Gee, I feel better all ready."

"I never was a Boy Scout," I said. "Come here."

Tiller turned toward the door and I thought he was leaving, but quickly he pulled a small revolver from his back pocket and shot four rounds through the front of the house. I flinched. Tiller reloaded the gun and walked off the porch toward me. I moved toward him.

"What the fuck are you doin' here?" he asked. "You tell me right now, or I'll fucking kill you."

"Why Tiller," I said. "You seem aggravated at your own house. Calm down. Like I said, I just came here to arrest your brother. And to give you a last chance to confess. Everybody deserves a last chance to confess their sins."

"Last chance or what!" he screamed. "Or what! What the fuck are you gonna do? Your law couldn't do shit before, and I beat your ass in court. You can't do shit now."

"Nothing, Tiller. I'm not going to doing a thing. Just asking you to do what's right. You can feel it. I know it."

Tiller looked at me in disbelief. And then he broke out laughing. The brothers laughed from the porch. "This game warden has come to our house, boys, to preach us a sermon. He's come to save our souls."

They laughed again. "Well," Tiller said. "How 'bout I do this. I'll protect myself from a crazy preachy game warden by sending you to your heavenly home."

"That ain't wise, Tiller."

"See this gun," he said holding it up for me to see. "You recognize it?"

I just looked at him.

"Took it from under yore ol' buddy Samuel's truck seat. He didn't mind, see, cause that son of a bitch was dead. And I bet nobody never noticed it was gone."

Samuel did carry a back-up Smith .38 Chief. It looked like his gun.

"This gun is the same gun that I took away from you after you shot at me. You missed and hit my house." He smiled. "Getting the picture now, Carp Cop. Done made the call to the sheriff. He's on his way now. Told him how you was crazy, waving a gun."

"That won't work," I said.

"Really? Why's that?"

"Cause anybody who knows me knows I don't miss," I whispered.

Tiller's lip quivered.

"Don't raise that gun, Tiller. Don't do it," I said.

"Or what? What are you gonna do? Send me to hell."

"I'm not going to do anything," I said.

Tiller smiled and began to raise the pistol. "I am," he said. "I'm gonna blow your head off, Carp Cop. And there ain't a thing you can do."

"No!" I yelled. I pointed to W.B.. "On the hill."

Tiller turned toward the hill and looked. "That hill? That way-far-away hill? Somebody on that hill? That what you're saying." He laughed. "You sure it ain't God on the hill and his angel is gonna strike me dead?" he said laughing. "I hate fuckin' game wardens," he said. And he pointed the pistol at my head and cocked the hammer.

The bullet struck him at the bridge of his nose, sending a frothing red-white cloud from the back side of his head. The impact of the bullet was strikingly loud, like slapping the water with a boat paddle and then I heard the report of the gun in the distance. Tiller's eyes were instantly dead. Instantly. No life in them. And he collapsed in an uncontrolled pile of flesh and bone.

Again, the loud slap of bullet striking bone emanated from a slightly raised second story window. The report of W.B.'s rifle wafted down the hill only to be clipped by a second shot exploding the second story window. Then, Sam was running toward me with the shotgun, covering the house. I dove for the truck and pulled the .45 from under the seat and turned as Edward Mabry raised a pistol and shot one round. The shot was strangely quiet, as I vaguely heard its report, but the bullet struck the side of the truck inches from my arm and that sound was very loud. I returned two shots, feeling the recoil of each shot. I remember the sights on his chest and squeezing the trigger as he took aim again and he collapsed on the porch, his legs quivering. The girl was screaming on the porch, hysterically wailing, with her hands over her head and then she dove for cover. The other two men were shooting from the side of the house and I could hear truck glass breaking as it fell to the ground and the sounds of tearing metal and then Sam tackled me and we hit the ground. "Take cover," he yelled. And I remember my back against the tire, and hearing Tom's shotgun and a man screaming and the zing of a bullet in the air over my head just as the man at the side of the house fell forward into the yard with his head almost gone and then I heard W.B.'s gun way far off in the distance. And then there was nothing, except the sound of us breathing and the girl whimpering.

I looked again at Tiller, his legs bent in unnatural positions with his torso and arms piled on top, like the air had been let out of him, deflated. I just sat there in the yard of that house, somehow peacefully disconnected, watching it all through my own tunnel vision.

I heard W.B.'s voice on Sam's radio. "Upstairs window on the right," he said. "He should be dead, but I'm not sure. You boys be careful."

Sam and I entered the house while Tom covered the window with the shotgun. Tom hand-cuffed the girl and left her whimpering against the wall. We moved through the house slowly, covering each section as we moved until we got to the upstairs bedroom where we saw Spike Mabry laying dead at a table at the window. There was a thirty-caliber carbine in his hands and the blood from his head wound had drained to the floor from the table top. When we emerged from the house, W.B. pulled into the yard in his truck. We gathered in a circle, everyone stern faced and serious.

"You all right, Ethan?" W.B. asked.

"Yeah," I said.

"Don't worry, Ethan. I got all of it up until the first shot, and then I left the camera running on the tripod."

"Where's Spike?" W.B. asked.

"Upstairs," Sam said. "He took one in the head. A bullet entered the stock of his rifle and kept going, too. He's dead. Still in a shooting position. Never moved a muscle, it looks like."

"Saw him stick the barrel out the window," W.B. said. "Couldn't really see the target, but figured he was at the end of the stock. That one was a bit tricky."

"Sam, call the TBI. Tell them we've had a shooting," I said. "Nobody touch anything and let those boys do their job. I'll call the office and report the incident. Remember, we don't talk to local law enforcement. Just the TBI. That's the procedure." We looked at each other. "Thanks, boys," I said. "I owe you all."

"No problem," Tom said. And the others nodded.

"And another thing," I said. "We're all ten-eight. On duty. I requested you to work this detail. Go turn the camera off."

W.B. lighted a cigarette. "Sons a bitches," he mumbled. "They would have killed you, Ethan. Made a game out of it."

I looked at the bloody pile that was once Tiller Mabry. "Are you okay, W.B.?"

W.B. glanced at the dead body. "Because of that?" he asked.

"Yeah."

"That idiot committed suicide," he said. "You told him. He didn't believe you. His mistake." W.B. stared at me. "Ain't never been called an angel of the Lord, before. Don't reckon that fits me."

"Me neither," I said. "Was worried you weren't hearing it all."

"Every word," he said. "We heard it all. This is on HIM," W.B. said with emphasis. "You didn't do a thing, Ethan. You hear me? The man killed himself."

"Well, he's dead. That's a fact," I said. There was a pause in our words. The reality of minutes past touched us and would not let go. "One last thing," I whispered. "We will all be interviewed today. We are not used to being interviewed. Tell the absolute truth. Hide nothing.

We have nothing to hide. We have done absolutely nothing wrong."

CHAPTER 25

An hour later, the scene was covered with law enforcement officers. The TBI lead agent was William Jackson, a good man I had known for ten years, certainly long enough to know he was concerned. His tie was loosened and his sleeves rolled up and stress lines accented his forehead. He led me over to his vehicle and we sat in his car. The inside of his unmarked Crown Vic had the faint smell of peaches.

"What happened, Ethan?"

"Is this the official interview, William?" I asked.

"No, that'll come in a bit," he said. "This conversation is between you and me."

I paused. "I'd rather you just review the tapes," I said. "It will be more accurate. I don't want to color it."

"You taped it?"

"Audio and video," I said.

"Why?" he asked.

"So there would be no misunderstanding about what I did. I violated no law, William. I just talked to the man."

"Why were you there?" he asked.

"I came to arrest his brother by orders of the judge and talk to Tiller."

"Talk to him?"

"Yes. Just talk."

He shook his head and sighed. "You had three officers strategically placed to cover you and document all your actions so you could talk to the man?"

"It took three."

"Do you use three armed officers to video your activities every time you talk to a man?"

"Only the ones who kill people," I said.

"You mean only the ones who kill game wardens," he said.

"That, too," I said.

"Okay…okay," he said. What happened?"

"He was gonna shoot me, and his brother upstairs leveled a rifle at me," I said.

"And you knew he might try something or W.B. wouldn't have been on that hill," he said.

"That's a true statement," I said. "I'm not hiding anything."

"If you knew Tiller Mabry might try to kill you, why would you want to talk to him? Why didn't you let the sheriff serve the warrant?"

I looked at him. "Cause the judge ordered me to arrest him, William. How's that?"

William sighed. "This is the damnest thing I've ever seen. I've never run across anything like this. Listen, this may get really weird, before it's over. You set this guy up, Ethan."

"How?"

"He had your friend killed and you killed him," he said.

"True," I said. "But only in self defense."

"But you maneuvered him into this?"

"You do your job, William. If I've messed up, I don't know how, but I know what your job is." I looked at him. "So do it."

"Okay," he said. "Here's how it'll work. We separate all the players now. We interview everyone. We hold W.B.'s rifle. We do forensics. We accumulate evidence. We turn it all over to the Attorney General. He makes the decision on whether there is probable cause a crime has been committed. If not, it's over. If so, it goes before the Grand Jury, and you know the rest of the story."

"I understand," I said.

"Between you and me. I have no feelings whatsoever for those scumbags on the ground out there. I have great respect for you and your men and the job you do. Hell, I wouldn't have your job. Alone, with these types, in the middle of the woods with no witnesses. That's crazy, but, the law is the law and I'm gonna do my job."

"That's why I've always liked you, William," I said.

He looked outside the window. I did the same. It was a beautiful April day with clear air.

"An officer goes to talk to a criminal and protects himself in case something goes wrong," he whispered to himself. "The conversation leads to an attempted murder and in self defense, all the bad guys die. How can something so simple be so complicated?"

"Because the perception is that I set the whole thing up to kill them," I said. "Because of vengeance for our friend they murdered. Just say it again."

William sighed again. "Okay. There'll be some who say it, but that's the thing. Set what up? A conversation? A failure to appear warrant. And even if you did, that's not illegal."

"Not to my understanding," I said. "How can something as simple as talking to a man and being prepared for violence cause such speculation of wrong-doing?"

"Everything goes back to intent, I guess" he said. "You did provide him with the perfect opportunity to die."

I smiled at him. "I provided him the perfect opportunity to confess," I said.

"Maybe you did," he said. "Who really knows why a man does anything?"

"God knows, I guess," I said.

"Agreed," he said quickly. "But I'm not sure if God's around today."

"If He's not," I said, "there was absolutely no reason for this conversation."

Chapter 26

She introduced herself with a firm handshake. Evelyn Atwood. About forty. Short brown hair. Slacks. Sig on her hip. Said she drove down from Nashville to do the interviews. She had saved me for last, which I expected. That's what I would have done. She said they always bring in unfamiliar agents to do interviews with other law enforcement. It was five p.m.

I had been in the interviewing room of the Sheriff's department many times, but never on this side of the table.

"I know it's been a long day," she started. "I'll make this as brief as possible."

"I appreciate that," I said.

"Have you contacted family members to let them know you are okay?" she asked.

"I'm alone," I said.

"No family?"

"Daughters, but I'll talk to them later," I said.

"Later may be too late. This is all over the airways. CNN and everything," she said.

"My girls are pretty tough," I said.

She shuffled papers in a file. "I've read your statement. I just have a couple of questions...You said that you were in charge during this incident. Correct?"

"Yes."

"Did you order Officer Langford to shoot Tiller Mabry?"

"No. I didn't have to. He is trained to protect other officers."

"Was there discussion prior to the event about shooting Tiller Mabry?"

"Yes."

"What was that discussion?"

"I asked Officer Langford what he thought Mr. Mabry would do if I confronted him with the death of Wildlife Officer Dooley. He said it depended on Tiller's mood. Officer Langford said that I should be clear about the fact that if Tiller attacked me, he would take the shot."

"Did you agree with Officer Langford?"

"I think I said that I hoped the day would end peacefully, but I certainly agree with his decision to take the shots."

"Did you go to the Mabry house to provoke a response?"

"Have you reviewed the tapes? Did I provoke him?"

"I'm asking the questions, Officer Stewart. Please answer. Was your intent to provoke a response that would end in Mr. Mabry's death?"

"My intent was to talk to the man and give him a chance to admit his wrongdoings and confess his crimes. Nothing more, and to arrest his brother for failure to appear."

"Again. Was your intent to provoke a response that would end in his death?"

"No, but if my answer was yes, the law allows me the right to protect myself from lethal attack with the same degree of force."

"Are you saying that you have the right to provoke an action that knowingly will end in death?"

"No, because no one can know what another will do in response to words. Truthful talk, by itself, is not illegal. Action can be illegal. If the truth, spoken in words, provokes illegal action, it must be the action that is responsible for the death, not the words."

She paused and looked at her notes. "You said, 'Give the man a chance to confess his crimes.' What crimes?"

"The murders of Oslo Janks and Officer Samuel Dooley."

"Mr. Mabry was not convicted of those crimes," she said.

"Have you listened to the tapes?" I asked. "He admitted taking the gun from Samuel's truck while he was dead. He said he hated game wardens. He said, 'I'm gonna kill you.' I stared at his eyes while he cocked the hammer and pointed that pistol at my head. Please, Agent Atwood, don't insult me."

"Didn't mean to," she said. "But nothing you just said would prove that Tiller Mabry committed murder."

"That's correct, but everything I just said leads to his action today to attempt to kill me."

She didn't flinch. "How did you know the whereabouts of this man called Slack? Is he dead?"

"I can't prove he's dead. Officer Langford received information from a confidential informant that this Slack guy was in fact the trigger man in the murders."

"You told Tiller Mabry that you knew about Slack and that he was dead and his body is in Kentucky Lake. You are telling me that you don't know if he's dead. Are you misleading me or did you mislead Tiller Mabry?"

"Neither. I wanted to watch his eyes when I told him what we had been told about Slack. I wanted to see his response."

"And what was his response? Do you remember?"

"Yes. For the first time in the conversation I believe he lied. He constructed his answer. He appeared deceptive."

"He then shot his own house, correct?"

"I think that's chronologically correct."

"Do you think, Officer Stewart, that your conversation with Tiller Mabry was responsible for his death and the deaths of all the men in that house today?"

"No. I think their threats on my life caused their deaths according to the rights I am afforded as a law enforcement officer for the State of Tennessee and as a citizen of this country to protect my life against threats of death, Agent Atwood."

For the first time she paused. "Officer Stewart, if you had not gone to the Mabry house this morning, would all these men still be alive?"

"Yes. I think they would be alive. But I did go to their house. I did confront them. My actions were perfectly legal. They chose to try to kill me. That's an illegal action. Their choice to violate the law by threatening my life is what killed them, Agent Atwood. Not my words."

"But you were deceptive, Officer Stewart. You gave them the scenario that you were totally alone, totally vulnerable."

"I sure did. Just like the TBI does and the FBI does and every tactical sting unit under cover. They present the idea of vulnerability….that everything is fine. And then you arrest them or kill them if they try to kill you. Why is this different? Because we are wildlife officers? Are we different?"

"But earlier, you said your words were truthful. You led him to believe you were alone. That is not truthful."

"I disagree," I said. "I told him there was an officer on a hill that had a gun on him. I told him I was not alone."

"Off the record, Officer Stewart, I wouldn't have believed that statement if I was Tiller Mabry."

"It was the truth," I said.

She smiled a bit for the first time and tried to charm me. "Are you that smart? That's what I keep asking myself. Am I dealing with a totally truthful man or a man that is very, very smart?"

I stared at her.

"You're not gonna answer that one, are you?"

She was right. I couldn't answer that question truthfully, because any answer was incriminating. I remained quiet.

"No, I didn't think so," she said. "I have never seen a case that looked so much like the whole thing was set up to kill them," she said. "And I assume the confrontation with Spike Mabry was also coincidental?"

"It was," I said. "I'm sorry it looks suspicious to you," I said. "The original confrontation with Spike Mabry was not set up."

She smiled for the first time and crossed her hands on the table. "I think that's all for now. Sorry for the questions, but we deal with them now or later. I hope dealing with them now will prevent the later scenario."

"I understand," I said. "No hard feelings."

Taylor was waiting. She met me in the yard and hugged me real hard. It felt good. She pulled away and looked me in the eyes.

"Don't say anything. Just look at me."

I did.

"You're okay, aren't you?"

"I am now," I said.

And we held each other for a long time in the darkness, hearing only the crickets, before going inside.

When we entered the house, John and Julia were sitting at the table. Julia stood and walked directly to me and buried her face in my chest and wrapped her arms around me. She held me for a long time. I watched John move to the stove and pour a cup of coffee. "Want a cup?" he said.

"No, John. I want a drink."

Taylor poured me bourbon and placed it on the table where I sat. She then sat next to me.

"You don't want one?" I said.

"Not tonight," she said.

John moved back to the table and sat with Julia. "Long day, huh?"

I laughed, but it didn't come out like a laugh. "Yeah," I said. "Long day."

My phone rang and I checked the number. "Hello."

"Dad," Abby said. "Are you all right?"

"Yeah, Abby. I'm fine."

"It's on CNN, Dad. There was shooting? Men died?"

"Yes. They did."

"And you were in the middle of it?"

"The middle," I said. "Yes, I was."

Taylor and John and Julia moved from the kitchen to the porch, leaving me alone, but Taylor paused at the door and looked back.

"Did you shoot somebody, Dad?"

"Yes. I did. Right after he shot at me."

"And he's dead?"

"I killed him," I said.

"And he shot at you?"

"Yes. Twice, I think."

"Then I'm glad he's dead. I'll be there tomorrow."

"No. No need, Abby. I'm fine."

"I know you're fine, Dad. You're always fine. You always handle everything. I'll be there tomorrow."

"You don't even know where I am?" I said.

"And you've forgotten who I am?" she said. "I'll find you."

"Listen to me, Abby. I want to see you, but not now. It will be very busy for a while and I prefer to see you when this settles down," I said.

She paused. "And you'll let me know?"

"I will."

"Then do, Dad. I'll be waiting."

"Thanks, Abby. I love you."

"I love you, Dad. Bye."

I closed the phone and watched it lay quietly on the table. I took a drink and stared at the phone again. It vibrated and I jumped.

"Hello."

"It's Amanda."

"Don't cry," I said. But she was.

"Are you okay?" she said. "You're not shot or bleeding or anything?"

"I'm not shot or bleeding or anything," I said.

"And they're all dead?"

"All of them," I said.

"Thank you, Ethan. Just thank you."

"For what?" I said.

Her voice broke again. "You don't know?"

"I'm not sure anymore," I said.

"Because you do what you say," she said. "And you're still a good man."

I swirled the bourbon in the glass. "Get on with your life, Amanda. Start fresh. It's over."

"I'll try, Ethan. I'll try."

"Good," I said.

"We love you, Ethan."

"I know. Goodnight."

And I turned the phone off and left it on the table. I found the others on the porch saying nothing. It was cool outside and the stars were shining and I sat next to Taylor. And no one spoke for a long time.

"Y'all can talk, you know," I said.

"We figured to just be with you and follow your lead on the talking stuff," John said. "Or, we can leave if you want to be alone."

"I would appreciate if you stayed," I said.

"You want to talk?" Taylor asked.

"Not sure what to say," I said. "Except we can rest now. John, you can quit toting the Colt; and Taylor, you can put the 870 back in the house; and Julia, you can quit looking in your rear view mirror for Spike. And maybe we can find some happiness in living a normal life."

"I've found a lot of happiness since I moved here, in spite of everything," John said.

"Funny how things happen," Taylor said.

"Free will's an amazing thing," I said.

"Yeah," Julia said. "My parents suck and so I move here. John's life was really hard, so he moves here. Ethan's life is very complicated and he moves here. And Taylor is the center of it. We all met here. Explain that one, somebody."

"Not me," Taylor said. "I'm just sure of one thing and that's that I'm not going anywhere. Especially now."

"It's a little more complicated than that," I said. "Taylor became your sister, Julia. That's why you came here. Her father built a great cabin on a creek. That's why I came here. Taylor is an amazing woman. That's why I stay here. John is family to a dear friend of mine, so he's my family too and I brought him here, 'cause I feel good here with Taylor and Julia. John likes it here, so he stays. I think Taylor likes us here, so she allows us to stay. Basically, none of us are going anywhere."

"Suits me," Taylor said. "I like it."

"Well," I said. "That's a good way to end this day, so I'm going to the cabin and sleep."

"You absolutely are not going to the cabin," Taylor said. "You're not going anywhere except to bed here. Nobody is sleeping in a separate house tonight."

"I really want a bed," I said.

"Take my bed."

I smiled. "I'm way too tired to argue. Thanks." And I said my goodnights and found my way to her bedroom, took a long shower and collapsed in her bed. And later in the darkness, when the thoughts of a bloody, lifeless Tiller Mabry were still fresh in my mind and sleep was impossible, the door to the bedroom opened and Taylor sat on the bed and took my hand.

"You asleep?" she whispered.

"Not even close," I whispered back.

Her weight shifted beside me.

"Don't leave," I said.

"You couldn't make me leave," she whispered.

And she walked around the bed and slid under the covers and I felt her arm around me and I took her hand and I felt her warmth against my chest and she moved her fingers to my face and traced the lines in my forehead and said, "Sleep…just sleep…or don't sleep. It doesn't matter. I'm here." And the memories of Tiller Mabry vanished, replaced with the soothing sound of her voice and the touch of her hand against my face.

"Thanks," I whispered.

And she said nothing, but squeezed my hand in the darkness.

"It's funny," I whispered.

"What?" she whispered back.

"I feel safest in the whole world with a little woman who drives a pick-up truck and listens to Jimmy Buffet."

"That's not funny," she said. "That's smart."

"You believe in kindred spirits?" I asked.

"I didn't before," she said. "But I do now."

Chapter 27

The next day I rose early, before the sun, and Taylor
was in the kitchen with coffee brewing. I sat at the table
and smiled at her.

"Did you sleep?"

She laughed. "Not a wink."

"Makes for a long day," I said.

"I'm used to it," she said sitting next to me.

"You slept," she said. "You snore a little bit."

"Sorry," I said.

"No," she said. "It's a cute little snore. Nothing bad."

"Your pillow smells like you," I said. "It's real nice.
You think I could borrow it for a while?"

She smiled. Her hair was freshly washed and it wasn't
quite dry and I thought her the most beautiful I'd ever
seen, even with no make-up. "That's sweet," she said.

"I'm a sweet guy," I said. "That's my real personality.
Sweet."

"I think that's true," she said. "Just a few get to see it though. So, what's on your agenda for today?"

The coffee was finished and I moved to the counter and poured a cup. "I have a meeting with the Attorney General, and then W.B. and I have to go through a psychological debriefing. You know, to make sure we're not overly stressed and depressed."

"Are you?" she asked looking up at me.

I leaned down and kissed her once, softly. "No," I said. "I'm not. Thanks."

"For what?" she asked smiling.

I sipped the coffee and smiled. "For being you."

Brian Alexander was the Attorney General. I had known him for thirty-five years. We played football against each other in high school and then we both went to U.T. We grew up in similar life styles: trained in the ways of the country, with back-up college degrees for our professional endeavors, but our real education was from country folk teachers.

I arrived at his office at nine. Lisa, his secretary, smiled as I entered as if nothing had happened.

"Want some coffee, Ethan?" she asked.

"No thanks, Lisa," I said.

"Come on in," Brian yelled from his office.

His office was in shambles, as usual. Files were stacked around the room with no apparent pattern of organization. There was an impressive smallmouth on one wall with a jig and pig hanging from its mouth and a bull canvasback on another wall centered among his diplomas and certifications.

"Sit down," he said.

"Well, am I in trouble?" I asked.

"I don't know," he said. "Are you? Jenny mad at you? Problems with the IRS? "

"What?"

"Just trying to determine how you could be in trouble," he said.

"Jenny passed away a year ago," I said.

He blinked. "Damn," he said. "Why doesn't anybody ever tell me these things? I'm sorry, Ethan. How?"

"Aneurysm, they say."

"I'm so sorry. She was…well, you know. She was special."

"Yes, she was, Brian."

He paused. "Well," he said. "Since this thing is all over the nation on T.V., I stayed up most of the night reviewing the evidence. Nothing I've seen or heard gives me any thoughts of wrongdoing on this Mabry deal."

"Glad to hear that," I said.

"Well, be prepared," he said. "The press is gonna eat your lunch and mine too, probably. Nashville papers been calling me all morning, as well as the TV stations."

"What did you tell them?"

"Nothing. Don't have to," he said. "Still under investigation, but I thought I'd end your suffering by letting you know. By the way, did you know the girl on the porch was an undercover cop?"

I was stunned. I looked at him. Took her three weeks to get in with them after the trial. You kinda blew that, Ethan, but she totally backed you."

I looked out the window.

"It would help if you really know the whereabouts of this Slack fellow," he continued.

"We have GPS coordinates of the location as supplied by our informant," I said. "I'll get them to you."

"Thanks," he said.

"Is it over?" I asked.

"Yeah, no cause for a Grand Jury investigation. Justified shooting in my book. There's the publicity thing, but as soon as I come out with my position, it should go away. It does look like you set the whole thing up, Ethan. Be clear on that. But on close review of the facts, I find no law has been broken and no crime committed. If I decided to prosecute you, I'd lose. I hate to lose, as you know. The whole thing is really interesting."

"What?"

"That if a law enforcement officer is smart enough to play a bad guy's psyche, he can make him commit a crime that will lead to his death, legally," he said.

I just looked at him.

"You did that, didn't you?" he said.

I just looked at him. "Nobody's that smart," I said.

"You are," he said. "And you got balls enough to do it."

He smiled at me. "I don't care, Ethan. The law is all I care about. If you can kill murderers legally, then have at it and until the law is changed, it's open season, as you boys would say."

I paused. "Just for conversation, how would a law be enacted to stop a person from being vulnerable and then protecting himself?"

"Can you spell gun control?" he said. "Same thing," he said. "Take away people's right to protect themselves and they are vulnerable and then can't protect themselves. You see, I can say that in the South and get away with it, 'cause it'll be after the war when Southern boys give up their guns."

I stood. "Thanks, Brian. I'll go tell the boys, if that's all right."

"That's fine. Tell them to remain quiet for a few days till it's official."

"I will."

"Oh, and one more thing. Agent Atwood, my best interviewer, I might add, says good guys are hard to find. Too bad they're all married, she said. I guess she saw the ring."

I paused at the door. "Good guys?" I said. "That's interesting."

CHAPTER 28

I arrived at the central office and saw W.B. sitting on the front steps drinking coffee from his Thermos. I sat next to him. Others passed, nodded, or said hi, but seemed to avoid us.

"How are you?" I said.

"Feel pretty rough," he said. "Trouble getting a good breath."

"How long has this been going on?"

"A while," he said. "Worse the last few days."

"Seen a doctor?"

He lit a cigarette. "Yeah, I talked to Doc Stone. He's the only doctor I've ever liked...hell of a bass fisherman...smallmouth mostly. Anyway, he said I need to go to Houston...some cancer center down there."

"You want me to take you?"

"Do I look like I need you to take me to Houston?"

"Thought you might like the company," I said.

"Kiss my ass," he said. "Stop with the pity shit."

"So, when ya going?" I said finally.

"As soon as we get through with this thing," he said. "I ain't going down there to get well, mind you. I just want to know how long I got and I figure they're the best at answering that question."

We sat without speaking.

"What if the treatment could cure you? Would you do it then?" I said.

"It can't," he said.

"You aren't sure of that. Miracles happen every day," I said.

"If miracles do happen, they can happen without tubes runnin' in my arm and me hairless and white-skinned and skinny," he said quietly.

"You're a tough guy. You could handle it, W.B."

"I am handling it, Ethan." He paused. "You ever wonder who'll show up at your funeral?"

I paused. "Never thought about it," I said.

"Interesting to ponder," he said.

I looked out across the yard. Bluebirds were feeding across the grass in little flashes of color. "Well, maybe this thing today won't take too long."

He smiled. "Unless you get blabby in there, won't last long at all."

I looked at him and smiled.

We entered the building as the Director was passing through the lobby. He stopped, walked to us and shook our hands, with meaning. "You boys okay?"

"We're fine, James," I said. "How are things at this end?"

"I got this end covered. Don't worry about the press. That's on me," he said. And he moved away, looking back. "But you're okay?"

"Yessir," I said.

We entered the main conference room and there were two people, an older man and a younger woman, at the front desk. They met our eyes and moved to us, shaking our hands. Bill and Sam, the undercover officers, entered the room and sat with us. We exchanged glances, but no words. We all waited. The older man started. Said he was a retired police officer from Nashville and had been involved in three shootings. He advised that it was necessary to talk about the incidents and feel free to talk about any feelings we had regarding the stress of ending a life and being shot at. He also said the discussions were confidential. The lady then introduced herself as a psychologist and offered her professional assistance.

"So, who wants to start?" the man said.

"I do," W.B. said. "I appreciate your concern for us, but this is the way I see it." His low voice concentrated attention in the room. "The first man I killed was holding a gun on my friend's head. The second piece of crap I killed was sitting in the window with a rifle pointed at my friend. I am pleased to have killed them under those circumstances."

The woman's eyes widened, having trouble comprehending W.B.'s emotion.

"Sir, are you a veteran?" she asked.

"I am," he said.

"And you have no second thoughts about what happened. No bad dreams or day dreams that bother you?" she said.

"I do," W.B. said. "Something is really bothering me."

"Talk about that," she said like she had broken through.

W.B. sighed and he paused a long time for emphasis. "My first bullet struck Tiller Mabry on the bridge of his nose from over four hundred yards distance. That is not where I wanted the bullet to strike. I wanted the bullet to enter his upper lip, just under the nose, in order to penetrate the base of the brain so his finger wouldn't spasm and shoot Ethan. As it turns out, the bullet placement was adequate; however, I regret that I miscalculated the number of clicks of elevation. I was three clicks high. That bothers me..."

We offered no comments, as we had nothing to add. The meeting was adjourned shortly thereafter.

Ella was waiting at my truck, her back against the fender with her arms crossed. She stared at me as I approached. I smiled, but she frowned and I prepared myself.

"Ella," I said. "You mad? You look mad."

"Shut up," she said.

I kissed her on the cheek.

"Don't do that!" She moved away. "People will think something," she said.

"People think what they want anyway," I said smiling. "I guess I'll kiss you if I feel like it. Hell, if you can't kiss one of your best friends in the whole world, who can you kiss?"

"A best friend doesn't walk out of the damn building after all you've been through and NOT stop by to say hello," she said. "So you can forget the best friend crap."

"I won't forget the best friend thing and don't ask me to," I said. "You know me. I'm no good at small talk and I didn't want to go up there and have to explain everything to the whole bunch in my old office. Besides, it would be strange going back up there."

She took a deep breath and looked at me.

"We're okay?" I said.

"We're always okay," she said.

"Even when you're mean to me?"

"Particularly when I'm mean to you," she said. "How are you?"

I paused. "Confused, maybe, I don't know."

"Meaning?" she said.

"I'm not sure," I said. "I thought things would make sense after the dust settled, but there doesn't seem to be a clear meaning."

"No satisfaction from murderers getting what they deserved?" she said.

I laughed quietly. "The world's a crazy place, Ella."

"Your damn right it's crazy. And so we keep fighting, I think," she said.

"Yep. That's what we do. We keep fighting," I said.

She smiled. "So, how's Miss Taylor James?"

I looked at her. "We're good."

"Really?"

"When I'm with her, I feel..." and I stumbled for the word... "right."

"Well," she said. "I hope she knows what she's got."

I looked at her. "You would be good friends," I said.

"So she knows how to give you a hard time?"

"Well, no one is as skilled as you in banter, but she can damn sure hold her own."

"Interesting," she said. "And W.B.? How's he doing after the incident?"

"W.B.'s dying," I said, looking away.

"What?"

"Lung cancer," I continued.

"I hear everything," she said. "I didn't hear that."

"Well, he doesn't talk a whole lot, you know," I said. "He refuses treatment, so it won't be a long illness."

"I'm sorry," she said finally.

"Don't be," I said. "That's what W.B would say anyway."

She moved away from the truck and looked back. "You'll do a better job of staying in touch, I hope."

"Yes, ma'am. I promise."

"See to it, Ethan. I mean it."

"Hey," I said.

She turned.

"If you died tomorrow, who would come to your funeral?"

She looked confused.

"Forget it," I said. "Just a thought."

"You would," she whispered,

I smiled at her. "Yes," I said. "I would."

CHAPTER 29

W.B. never came back from Houston. He never said goodbye when he left and he never called from Texas. Doc Stone from Humphreys County called late at night and gave me the news W.B. was never coming home, and added he had lost the best smallmouth fishing partner of his life. I think he was crying.

I didn't cry. I was shocked that W.B died that quickly, and I felt an emptiness, and maybe even sadness. I'm not sure. I had never known another man like W.B.

When I told John the next morning, he looked wounded and I wanted to hold him, but it seemed awkward, so we just stood there in the back of Taylor's yard with the cardinals sounding, and finally he called his dogs and walked away. I remember thinking that even the dogs acted sad as they walked away with John, sensing his mood.

When I told Julia and Taylor, Julia wanted to go after him, but I told her it best to give him space. Taylor just looked at me and smiled, like she knew what I felt and I sort of smiled back and left them, returning to my cabin, the entire time wishing she was with me. She called later.

"You ok?"

"Sure," I said.

"Anything I can do?"

"You just did," I said.

"It's not much," she said.

"Yes, it is. It's much for me," I said.

We had a memorial service for W.B. two nights later at the Short Creek Baptist Church. The church held about two hundred people, but that seating wasn't enough, so we moved everyone out to the yard under the oaks and sat on the ground. They were country folks mostly, dressed in a variety of backwoods fashion. W.B would have liked the lack of formality in the service, as people just stood and talked whenever they felt the urge. The stars were clear that night and the wind was calm, making it easy to hear the words.

I learned much about W.B. Langford that night…mostly that kindnesses your friends extend to others may never be talked about. We should be not so quick to judge others based on our own conversations, I think.

There was an elderly woman who said she first met W.B. when she had a flat tire on a gravel road out on Long Branch and W.B stopped to help her out. She lived alone after her husband died, and she allowed that W.B. never missed a week after the tire changing that he didn't check on her and fix stuff around her house. She said he even mowed her yard.

Another man said he always liked W.B. 'cause he was always the same. Tough. That brought a laugh. And we really laughed when he told the story of W.B "whupping" his ass one night when he was drunk and picked a fight. Said W.B. could have given him a ticket for illegal coon hunting, but said after the ass "whupping" that he had punished me enough.

Usually, at a service of that sort, fellow officers speak the most. Not that night. By the time the thirty or so people gave testimony to W.B.'s life, we had little to do but smile. Toward the end, the guys nudged me to speak for them, and I rose. I always have words. Always. But this night, I was searching.

"W.B. Langford was a man of his word," I said. "If he said it, with that low voice, it was the truth, at least his truth. And he was our brother. A good brother. We are proud of our brother and the life he lived. And we will miss him."

I sat and Taylor took my hand. But she took my arm when John Russell rose to speak. I looked at her face and she was teary, with lips that trembled as she watched the young man stand and address the crowd. Julia stood beside him and shored him up and we could tell that he took strength from her touch.

"When my Mom and I were struggling, he was there. When I wanted to learn about being a man, he was there. When I was alone, he was there. And when he couldn't be there, he sent his friend. I love my real father, but I have no memories of him 'cause he died when I was a baby. But I've had several men who looked after me, as a father would. W.B. Langford was one of my fathers. And

I'm lucky he was. I'm real lucky and I won't ever forget it either...I will always have strong memories of W.B. Langford."

No one spoke after John, but everyone remained seated for a long time and we listened to the night. Later, Doc Stone presented me a hand-made walnut box, with much the same curl of a premier gunstock, and said that W.B. wanted the ashes scattered under Name Rock on Hurricane Creek. He also said that W.B. asked that I be the executor of his will. I smiled and took the box, noting immediately how light it was. Ashes don't weigh much. Memories are real heavy, I thought.

CHAPTER 30

The next morning, sitting on the porch of the cabin, I watched the sun come up over White Oak Creek, with its ripples and blue holes running in some natural life of continuance. Berit nuzzled my hand and forced me to rub her head and she shut her eyes in a wonderful dog-exclamation of true love. I felt her warm breath on my fingers. The crows were calling in the distance and the coffee tasted strong, like I want it to taste.

There was nothing I could do to hold it back. A force of such attachment to things unsaid or refused or laid back or delayed, rushed me at the same instant I felt the complete loyalty of my friend, my simple dog, who never asked for anything except a touch of my hand or a kind word.

The dog looked up when my body began jerking and she whined when I sobbed and she attempted to climb into my lap and I dropped the mug of coffee and held her like a child and she whined with my sobs, licking my hand and wagging her stubbed tail, barking once to attack the thing that held me. And all the things that had held me prisoner over the last year were there on that porch, and my only weapons were cries and an ugly dog fighting an unseen enemy of grief.

I never cried after losing Jenny, not even at the funeral. I knew it dangerous to lose my control. The same with W.B. Perhaps it was time. I was lucky to have such an unselfish friend that smelled of dog hair and earth. She asked for no words to explain. Good thing. I had no words…

In the afternoon, John Russell and I drove to Hurricane Creek and wound our way through the woods to Name Rock. The view was spectacular, overlooking the Tennessee River, looking south past Danville, past Cane Creek and White Oak and in the far distance, Turkey Creek. From the rock we could see maybe fifteen miles of blue water and forests. Stories were told of old Jack Hinson taking vengeance on Union troops with his long rifle from this rock, picking off riverboat officers from six hundred yards. Seems the northern troops killed his two sons for hooliganism and Jack declared a one man war, stopping traffic on the river for a long time, troops fearing the father's shooting ability. No wonder W.B. found kinship with the place.

We studied the rock, with hundreds of names carved on its surface with old dates of "1863" and names like "Hinson," with the "S" etched backwards.

"Ever been here?" I asked John.

"Once," he said. "He brought me up here. We were hunting morels one spring."

"Fitting place for him," I said.

"Yes, it is," he said, never taking his eyes from the rock.

"You looking for something particular," I asked.

"Here," he said and pointed.

I looked. It was a recent etching. I studied the letters and looked back at John.

"He did it," John whispered.

"Who?"

"W.B.," he said. "I watched him carve her name."

I looked back at the name.

L O U I S E

"Did he explain?"

"Well, kinda," he said. "As best as W.B. could, I guess. Said she was a wonderful woman who lived in the most beautiful place in the world. Said she lived in a neat little caboose with two dogs and a horse in the mountains of northern New Mexico and looked after a property for the owner. Said she carried a Colt single action and was good with it. That's all he said."

And we stood there for a long time listening to the wind swirl and the leaves rattle in the trees around us. Finally, I moved to my pack and took out the walnut box.

"Never done this before," I said. "Not sure the proper method."

"I'd like the box, if it's okay," he said, "after you're through."

"Sure," I said. And I removed the lid, staring into the ashes and bone chips that once were our friend.

"So long, old friend," I said. And I scattered the ashes into the wind over the bluff and the wind caught them and swirled them around in a gray dusting that clung to the leaves and sailed farther over the view of the river. John said nothing, and after a while, I handed him the box and he took his fingers and ran them around the inside of the box. He then removed them, all gray-stained with ash and pressed his fingers against his forehead and drug them across his skin, leaving a mark of W.B. Langford on his face.

"What's that?" he whispered looking into the box.

"What?" I said.

"Look," he said handing me the box.

There were two sets of numbers scribbled in the wood in the bottom of the box. Definitely W.B.'s writing.

"They were under his ashes," John said. "What are they?"

"Probably nothing," I said. "He probably had the box for years and liked it and wanted his ashes in it, but you can't ever tell what the box was used for before."

"What could they be for?"

"Oh, I know what they are," I said.

"What?"

"They are GPS coordinates, John."

On the way home we stopped by the Danville boat ramp to make a game warden appearance. No objective. Just being seen. It's a wonderful tactic to make things happen or find out information. Probably eighty percent of all cases are made just driving around hoping something will pop up. It usually does.

A commercial fisherman was loading his boat on his trailer as we approached. He was a broad, short man with a full beard and he glanced up as we closed the distance, then repositioned a net in the boat, attached the bow to the trailer rope hook, pulled it tight with the winch and walked back toward his truck.

I waved friendly-like, and he nodded, and then raised a finger toward me meaning wait a minute. I cut the Jeep engine and waited a minute. Then I got out and so did John as he pulled the boat out of the water, parked, and walked toward us.

"You know me?" he asked.

"No, sir," I said. "Should I?"

"Do you, son?" he asked John.

"No, sir."

"Good," he said. "I need to talk to Mr. Stewart alone."

"No problem," John said and moved away from us toward the lake.

"I was a friend of W.B. Langford," he said. "He always treated me with respect. What's your feeling about commercial fishermen?" he asked.

I smiled. "Just like anything else," I said. "There's good ones and bad ones."

"That weren't my question," he said. "You gave me an observation. I'm looking for your feelings."

"You do a valuable job of removing rough fish from the waters," I said. "The fact that you make money doing it doesn't bother me near as much as tournament bass fishermen making big money with corporate sponsors and claiming to never hurt the fish, at the same time slamming you for making a living working real hard in bad weather all the time. Is that feeling enough for you?"

He smiled. "I heard you were a fair man," he said.

"I try," I said. "Truth is the truth."

"Sometimes I hear stuff," he said. "What I heard yesterday bothers me."

"What did you hear?"

He lit a Camel with a scarred ZIPPO and spit out a piece of tobacco. "There is a man. You'll know him when you see him, cause he don't fit in around here. He's gonna kill you, Mr. Stewart, if he can."

I paused. "That is bothersome. Any reason you know of?"

"That's all I'm saying, but it has something to do with money that Tiller gave you to do something and you didn't."

"Tiller gave me money?" I said. "That's ridiculous."

"Didn't say it was right. Just said that's what I heard."

"I have a question," I said.

"Okay."

"The chance of me coming by here today and meeting you is almost non-existent. If I hadn't stopped by, would you have contacted me?"

He smiled. "Can't rightly answer that truthfully," he said. "All I know is you did see me today and I did tell you. I figure it divine, but then I'm a believer, Mr. Stewart, so that might not make sense to you. I figure God was toying with me to call you, but knew I was weak, so he delivered you here today. When you pulled up I nearly lost my breakfast."

"I see," I said. "You know I have to ask you how you know this thing."

"I know. All I can say is they tried to get a local feller to do the job and he told 'em to kiss his ass. Then they said they'd kill his family if he blabbed."

"So he blabbed to you," I said.

"Telling me ain't blabbing," he said. "He knew I'd somehow get word to you in a quiet way."

"Cause you're a good man," I said.

"Naw," he said. "Cause the Lord's got a hold of me these days. That's all."

"And you're not gonna tell me your name," I said.

"Saw you lookin' at my boat numbers," he said. And then he smiled. "Got 'em memorized yet?"

I smiled back at him. "Sure I do."

"Good, cause I borrowed the boat and truck today. Lord told me to."

CHAPTER 31

In the truck, John said nothing.

"Awful quiet," I said.

"Waiting for your lead," he said.

"Put your gun back on," I said.

"Okay," he said. And that was all he said.

"Don't you want to know why?"

"Only if you want to tell me," he said.

"I will when I know something," I said. "Write down those numbers for me, will you?"

"The box numbers?"

"Yeah, the numbers in W.B.'s box."

"Okay," he said again.

"And let's keep the girls out of this for a while," I said. "No need worrying them until it's time for them to worry."

"Okay," he said. "I thought it was over."

"Me, too, John. Me, too."

"I'm beginning to think trouble never ends," he said.

"Well, if we lived in a subdivision in Nashville and sold software for a living, maybe that kinda life would be less stressful."

"Naw," he said. "There'd be something."

Later that afternoon, I was sitting on the bank of Cane Creek watching redhorses scoot up the shoals. Watching fish in the creek always improved my deductive reasoning. I retrieved my cell phone and punched in Sam, the spook's, number. I figured he wouldn't answer. Probably undercover in the mountains again. On the fifth ring, he said, "Yeah."

"It's Ethan. Where are you?"

"Driving. I'm alone. What's up?"

"You remember you told me about a seven hundred and fifty thousand dollar pay off to Tiller Mabry?"

"Yeah."

"What was it for?"

"Front money for the buying of eggs for the Russians," he said.

"Did we ever follow it after Tiller got it?"

"No. Why?"

"I just had a guy tell me there's a hit on me because Tiller convinced somebody that I was on the take and he had paid me money," I said.

Long pause. "That ain't good," he said. "If Tiller wanted to really get you, he could convince the Russians he paid you to do something, like, I don't know, pay off judges or something. You with me?"

"Yes. But if he told them that, and I didn't follow through with whatever the hell he told them I was supposed to do, wouldn't they expect him to correct it?"

"Yeah," he said. "But you got a problem."

"What?"

"Tiller's dead, Chief."

"Oh," I said, feeling stupid. "I see."

Taylor came in the cabin at dusk carrying pizza. Berit met her at the door and wagged and sniffed and nuzzled until Taylor put the food down and addressed her properly. Once satisfied that the lady still loved her, Berit jumped on the couch and collapsed, put her head on her feet and was close to sleep in ten seconds.

"You've stolen the affection of my dog," I said.

"Absolutely," she said. "My plan all the time. Loving Berit has helped with the loss of Jasper."

I paused a beat at the mentioning of her dog. "Want a drink?"

"Sure," she said. "Whatever you are drinking."

So I made her a drink at the bar and watched her unbox the pizza and place it on a platter. She wore faded jeans and a white pullover and I thought that no model in any catalogue could compare with the way she wore her clothes. Hands down winner.

"You look nice," I said handing her the drink.

"Thank you," she said. "Hungry?"

"Always," I said. "Started eating at an early age and grew to enjoy it."

We sat on the couch with Berit and she looked up briefly and then moved to put her head in Taylor's lap. The dog let out a long sigh like she was at the end of something exhausting, but we both knew it was ultimate contentment.

"We said we were always going to be open and truthful," she said.

"Yes, we did," I said.

"So," and she turned to look at me. "When we were going through the recent stress of Tiller Mabry and you stayed at the big house as you call it…" and she stopped.

"And?"

"I don't know. If I say it, then it becomes less of a thing, because you should have brought it up and now I'm not sure I should finish."

"Then I will."

"I doubt it," she said.

"Wanna bet?"

"No."

"When we were staying together at the big house we were very close, even if stressed and scared. And now, with the days more normal, I'm back at the cabin and normal is less intense. And you are wondering if the feelings are the same."

"Why did you make me bring it up?" she asked. "Why did you move back here? I didn't ask you to."

I swallowed the bourbon and tried to smile. "The truth is I'm not sure. Never been here before. I don't want to mess us up. I don't want to go too fast. I don't want to assume feelings you may or may not have."

"You won't if we talk. In the beginning it was you doing all the talking and I was the shy one, trying to figure you out."

"Did you figure me out, Taylor?"

"Yeah. All I need to know," she said.

"When?"

"The night you wouldn't leave me when my dog died and you held me all night around a campfire. You knew how bad that hurt. You knew. And you didn't try to lessen it or try to explain it away because you knew it wouldn't just go away." She placed her hand on my leg and I felt the warmth of her hand on my jeans. She looked into my eyes and talked with them. Berit looked up at her movement and left us on the couch and collapsed on the floor and stretched. "The night you gathered us all into the house and said no one was leaving because you had to have us close to protect us. The night you let me sleep with you and hold you after that terrible day and that was all you wanted that night, was to have me hold you." And she paused and then smiled. "The night you asked me what song was in my CD player..."

"Shut up," I said. And I placed my drink on the coffee table and took her hand, leaning close to her face and those eyes that talked to me. "Come here," I said.

"I am here," she whispered.

"No. Come here," and I pulled her closer and I gently kissed her and our hearts were pounding and I could feel it in her lips and our breathing was quickened. And somewhere in my vision I saw the dog look up quizzically, as we continued with more feeling until she playfully pulled away and rested her head on my chest.

"Wow," she said.

"I think we have confused the dog," I said.

Taylor whisper-giggled. "As soon as I get my breath, she ain't seen nothing yet."

"Wow," I whispered.

CHAPTER 32

I reluctantly got up before sunrise the next morning and drove to Nashville, entering the office a bit before eight. The cleaning lady was vacuuming the Director's office and she smiled pleasantly and called me by name. I smiled back as James entered the room with a cup of coffee.

"Mornin'," he said.

"Good morning, James. Got a minute before you start your day?"

"Sure. Come on in. Shut the door," he said. "I brought donuts."

They were all chocolate covered, sitting on his desk. He promptly plucked one and was eating while taking his seat.

"No choice, I see. Chocolate or chocolate," I said.

"Why put people in the trick?" he said. "Everybody wants chocolate anyway. Why make them make that choice so early in the day?" He licked his fingers.

"As always," I said. "You are one step ahead."

"Hmm," he said.

"According to protocol, I'm supposed to report a threat against an officer," I said.

"Who?"

"Me, but I have no clue as to its seriousness."

He chewed some more and swallowed and followed it with coffee. "Okay," he said. "Give me a best and worst case scenario."

"Best is some kin of Tiller is trying to scare me."

"Are there any left? Thought they were all dead. No offense," he said.

"Genetics is a far-reaching thing in backwoods Tennessee," I said. "Worse case is the Russian mafia."

"Hmm," he uttered again. "Why them?"

"My information is that Tiller told the Russians that he paid me off to do some unknown thing to help with the paddlefish market. And, I didn't do this thing, so the Russians want their money back or me dead."

"How much money?"

"Seven hundred and fifty thousand dollars."

"That's enough," he said. "And after all, you aren't really the police, just a game warden in a hick town. So it's not like they would be taking on the FBI," he said.

"Yeah, there's that," I said.

"Want another one?" he said motioning to the donuts.

"No thanks," I said.

"I think I should make some calls," he said.

"Maybe that would be good," I said. "Just to see what some federal departments may know about this thing."

"Maybe I do more than that," he said. "And maybe you should get lost for a while."

"No," I said. "I'll be watchful."

He sighed and looked out the window before back at me. "And vigilant, too."

I smiled. "Yessir. That too."

"I'll let you know if I find anything helpful," he said. "Watch your back, Ethan. In the end, we still have the same old goal. You remember our old friend's motto?"

I smiled. "Yeah, live long enough to piss out their tracks. Always thought that motto a bit crude," I said.

"Yeah. So was our old friend. But he sure knew how to get things done."

"That would be correct," I said.

On the way upstairs I visited with people I once worked with daily and thirty minutes later I entered my old office. It was empty except for Ella, who was standing at the window, looking outside.

"Hey," I said, and she turned. She paused for a second, staring at me, and then walked toward me. "What? No smile? No hug?" I said.

"What do I look like? Huh? A cheerleader?" she said.

I sat across from her desk. "No, cheerleaders are always 'cheerful'," I said.

"Yeah, and for the most part, stupid," she said sitting. "Do I look stupid to you?"

"No," I said. "You look pissed, and for the life of me, I can't figure out why?"

"Why? Why! How 'bout the fact that just twenty minutes ago the Director calls up here to get 'at least one' covert guy off whatever the hell they are doing to come shadow you until further notice. How about that 'why'?" she said.

I shook my head. "It's nothing," I said.

"You listen to me, Ethan Stewart. I am the Chief's secretary. I still know everything. Everything goes through me and you know why, because I am trusted to keep my mouth shut when I need to be discreet. I know about the threat and I know about the Russians."

"I know you know everything. I generally count on it," I said. I looked around. "Where is everybody?"

"Everybody is scrambling, as of twenty minutes ago, to get you a tail, so if somebody offs you, they can kill the bad guy."

"Well, for the record, I'd appreciate their involvement before the offing," I said.

"You and I both know it rarely works that way. What have you got yourself into, Ethan?"

"A smart old man once tried to explain it to me, Ella, but I didn't quite get it," I said.

"What?"

"Had something to do with ants," I said.

"What!!"

"Whoa. Calm down. Just answer me this question 'cause it's all that matters to me at this very second," I said.

"What?"

"You still with me?"

She frowned, then stared, and finally her eyes lit up and she smiled real big. "More than ever," she said. "I love all this excitement and this is the way it used to be around here all the time when you were here," she said. "I miss it. I miss you."

I stood, leaned across the desk and kissed her forehead. "That, my dear friend, is all I need to know."

I paused at the door. "So, you're not really concerned with my survival?"

"Hell, no," she said. "You wouldn't dare leave me."

I smiled at her "Ella" way of thinking. "I do miss you," I said.

"You'd be crazy not to," she said smiling.

I picked up the friendly tail in Dickson. I stopped at a convenience store and he was waiting in a rusted out Chevy truck when I came out. His window was down and I said "Hi," as I passed. His name was Chuck and I hadn't seen him in about a year. Quiet guy who would rarely talk, but one hell of a pistol shot. He always carried a Walther PPKS .22, loaded with Stingers. Said nobody would suspect him being the law carrying a .22. Chuck touched the brim of his hat as I passed and said nothing.

In Erin, I stopped at Mary's for lunch. I parked the green state truck outside in plain view, went inside and picked a corner table with my back to the wall. I had no plan at all except to remain in plain sight and see what happened.

The lunch crowd left an hour later and my waitress was very good about refilling my coffee. I finally told her that I was waiting for a friend and it might be a while.

A black Tahoe with tinted windows passed three times in thirty minutes and finally stopped. No movement for ten minutes. And then two men, both wearing black, got out and started toward the door. They both had jackets draped over their right hands and I touched my Kimber that was tucked under my left leg. I looked at them entering the restaurant and turned the page of the Nashville Tennessean in front of me on the table.

The waitress met them and said "hi, y'all", but they never acknowledged her presence and made their way to my table, where they stood towering above me. Both men were tall and the one on my left was muscled up and dumb-looking strong.

"Ethan Stewart?" the one on my right said with a clipped accent.

"Who's asking?" I said.

"I ask," he said.

"Sit down, boys," I said. "I'm Ethan Stewart."

They sat, each resting their arms on the table, right hands under the coats.

"What can I do for you?" I said.

"You have money from that baboon Tiller Mabry. Give us money, we kill you and spare your family. You don't give us money, we kill you now and your family later. Simple."

"Is this the part where I wet my pants and start begging for my life?" I asked.

The talker looked at his friend and smiled. "We have real American cowboy."

"Fun we have here," the muscle said smiling.

"Tiller Mabry lied," I said. I had the Kimber pointed at the big man under the table, thinking the talker was less prepared to pull the trigger.

"No matter," the talker said. His left hand was fingering a fork on the table. Tattoos were visible on his little finger, ring finger, and index finger. Letters I could not recognize. "We kill you anyway."

"Right now?" I said. "You would kill me here in plain view of everyone?"

He laughed. "This place is nothing," he said. "It is nowhere place. Last chance. Where is money?"

"I have a question," I said. "You have guns under those coats?"

The big man took his left hand and pulled the coat exposing the barrel of a large bore pistol.

"I see," I said and I pulled the trigger. The report was deafening and my ears rang as the bullet angled upwards through the table. I saw his chin move backwards with blood and I shot twice more toward the talker and the glass behind me shattered and I rolled to the ground. The talker was hit and staggered backwards, firing randomly in my direction, as he stumbled once across a table. I shot as he stood, catching him in the upper chest, but he did not go down, and he turned to run. Chuck was standing at the door and I heard his little .22 bark twice, and the man instantly collapsed and rolled toward me. I looked at his face and there was a small hole above his right eye and massive blood where his left eye used to be. Returning to the first man, I saw a pool of blood around his head, his vacant eyes staring toward the ceiling.

"You all right, Chief!" Chuck yelled.

"Yeah," I said. "Any other vehicles outside?"

"No," he yelled. They were alone."

I saw the waitress standing behind the counter to our right with her hands over her mouth and the cooks were gawking from the back. And everything was very quiet, except the sound of my heart pounding in my ears. I reloaded a fresh magazine and leaned against the wall. "Damn," I whispered to myself. I saw Chuck remove the magazine in his little gun and replace it with a fresh one and back himself against the wall looking outside.

CHAPTER 33

I talked with Taylor after the shooting and assured her I was fine, but it would be awhile before I returned home. She tried real hard to be brave, but I could tell the strain was getting to her. She said John was with her and refused to let her or Julia out of his sight. She asked if this nightmare would ever end. I told her the truth. "Eventually," I said. The truth was I knew almost nothing about the genetics of the Russian mafia.

Four hours later, I finished the interviews with the T.B.I. and there was a big difference between this time and the last. Two Russian mobsters. Two guns. A link with Tiller Mabry. It was a formality interview.

I met Chuck outside the Sheriff's Department at his rusty Chevy. There were five Wildlife Officers standing around for support.

"Everything go okay, Chief?" one asked.

"Yeah, pretty cut and dried," I said. "Now this guy," and I shook Chuck's hand. "This guy can shoot."

He smiled a bit and I didn't think he would say a word, but he kind of whispered. "Just glad I didn't have to shoot my guy through a table."

"Let's go home. How 'bout it?" I said.

"Chuck's coming with us," one said. "He needs a drink."

"Y'all be careful," I said.

My mind was racing on the drive home. My phone rang and Taylor's voice was serious. "There is an F.B.I. agent here to see you."

"Is he in the house?" I asked.

"Yes."

"Did he show you identification?"

"Yes."

"Can he hear you talking now?"

"Yes."

"I want you to laugh right now like I said something funny," I said.

There was a pause. And then she laughed.

"Now say, okay."

"Okay," she said.

"Tell him I'll be there in ten minutes," I said.

"Okay."

Now my mind was really racing. Why not see me at the interview? How did he know where I live? Why not call me instead of showing up at my home? I called back to the Sheriff's office and ask for the T.B.I. Agent, William Jackson.

"William."

"Yes."

"Ethan. Is the F.B.I. in on this already?"

"Why?"

"There is an F.B.I. agent waiting for me at my house," I said.

"That was quick," he said.

"So they are involved?"

"Yes, Ethan. This is big."

"Okay," I said. "Just checking."

I parked my truck behind the gray Crown Vic in the driveway. Three antennas. Civilian plates. I wrote the number down on a pad before leaving my vehicle.

I entered the house without knocking and he was sitting in the foyer drinking a cup of coffee. John was standing ten feet away, leaning against the wall.

I immediately extended my hand. "Ethan Stewart," I said.

He carefully placed the coffee cup on a table and stood.

"Agent Smithson." He shook my hand. "Sorry to barge in like this, but we need to talk," he said.

"May I see some I.D.?" I said.

He took it from his jacket pocket and I saw his service weapon holstered professionally on his right hip. Cocked and locked. I carefully examined the credentials. Authentic. I returned them and looked at John.

"Girls all right?"

"Yes, sir."

Back to Smithson. "Never known an F.B.I. Agent to show up solo," I said. "Usually you guys come in pairs."

He smiled confidently. "You are observant. My partner is stuck in weather at O'Hare. I was already in the area."

"Well, Agent Smithson, I've had a really tough day and I'm wondering why this couldn't wait until tomorrow."

"When we talk, you'll understand," he said.

"Fair enough," I said. "Let's go down to my place. I need a drink. Want to follow me?"

"Sure," he said. To John he said, "Please tell Miss James thanks for the coffee."

"Yes sir. I will."

"And John," I said. "Don't forget to feed the dogs."

He paused a beat. "I will," he said.

The ugly dog barked at my guest when we entered the cabin, but quickly recovered when I let her out to rid the yard of goblins.

"Unusual looking dog," Smithson said.

"But a beautiful heart," I said making my way to the bar. "Make yourself at home," I said and he seated himself at the kitchen table, back against the wall. I studied him while I built the drink. He had salt and pepper hair, cut close to his head. Maybe fifty. Several old scars on his face. Thick fingers and broad hands. He was maybe an inch shorter than me, but heavier. No fat. And absolutely serious. His presence was intimidating because there was nothing resembling incompetence about him. Not many men I had ever met scared me. He did. "Want a drink?"

"No thanks," he said.

I moved to the kitchen sink and remained standing. "I'm all ears," I said.

"Do you have any idea who tried to kill you today?" he asked.

"Nope," I said. "They aren't from around here I bet."

"No. They are not," he said. "Actually, those two were residing in Atlanta for the last year. But the family has been in New York for a number of years. That's where the father runs several illegal businesses…drugs, prostitution, guns, money laundering, and the list goes on."

"The father?"

"Yes," he said. "You killed his youngest son today."

"Actually, I killed his body guard. My partner killed the son, I would bet."

He smiled. "Well, he is dead. And that is the point. The son was a screw-up, failing in all the businesses his father tried to set up for him, so his latest venture was to allow the son, name of Nikoli, by the way, to establish a business of cornering all the paddlefish egg buying on Kentucky Lake to replenish the flailing Russian caviar supply."

"Enter Tiller Mabry," I said.

"Correct. Seems the locals wouldn't do business with foreigners, particularly Russians, and Tiller saw an opening to be the liaison. Then things went bad in a hurry. You killed Tiller. No liaison. No egg buying. And the money sent to start the business is gone. The father was furious. The son embarrassed. The son comes here to restore his reputation with his father…get the money back and kill you for causing him the problem. You know, get back in his father's good graces. "

"I'm still at a loss about why this is so important for me to know," I said.

"You killed his son. You stole the father's money. It's an honor thing," he said.

"I stole nothing," I said.

"Explain this then," he said. "They didn't trust Tiller, so a transmitter was hidden in the money to track it. The money, or at least the transmitter, was stationary from the time Tiller took possession until two weeks ago. The transmitter died three weeks ago. Right before Tiller's death. He claimed he gave you five hundred thousand. That you were his partner to assure no legal problems with the harvest of the eggs."

"How could you possibly know all these details?" I said. "You either have a hell of surveillance system on them, or you are a fraud."

He smiled and looked me straight in the eyes. He smoothed the table cloth with his hand and calmly continued. "Now, before you try anything irrational, know this. I am very good at my job."

"Which would be killing people?" I said.

"Sometimes," he said. "But I was actually hired by the father to watch Nikoli while he was down here, and tidy things up if he failed. Well, he failed pretty quickly. And I don't operate remotely like the Russians. They are very clumsy. Barbaric actually. I have survived for many years in this business doing things in a very organized manner with little room for error. There is no reason for us to be violent or cause harm to anyone. It can be arranged if need be, you understand, but it is not necessary."

"Damn fine forgeries of your I.D."

"It's amazing what lots of money will buy," he said.

"I mean, I am impressed," I said. "Your vehicle. Your clothes. Your weapon. Your demeanor. Very good."

"Well, like I said, I've been at this a while and I am always successful, which means I am very expensive, an impeccable reputation and the go-to-guy for difficult work. I only operate at a, shall we say, upper level."

"Upper level in backwoods Tennessee," I said. "The locals would be flattered." I crossed the room and sat at the table across from him.

"So, I have a gun and you have a gun and you are not the least bit worried about the fact that I am kind of in a shooting mood today?"

"Not the least bit worried. You are very smart. I've studied you. You are very cool under pressure. Your tactical methods with Tiller Mabry were unique and," he laughed, "beautiful. You allowed the man to kill himself without his knowledge."

"At least I have your respect," I said.

"You do," he said. "And I don't ever say that. It's quite rare to find someone like you."

"I am curious," I said. "Isn't what you do tiring? I mean when do you rest?"

"Aren't all jobs tiring," he said. "And I sail. That is restful."

"How big is your boat?"

"Not that big," he said. "Thirty-five feet. I sail alone. As you would expect. I have no friends."

"Around here, that is big."

"What? Having no friends or the boat?"

"Both are big," I said. "And the friend thing is very sad."

He shrugged. "I think I will have a drink," he said. "Just a small one."

"You see the bar. Build it to your own liking. That way you won't think I poisoned you," I said.

He got up and moved to the bar. "Never crossed my mind," he said.

I went to the fireplace and struck a match to start a fire, the wood waiting. It cracked and smoked a bit while starting up. I sat in the den and waited for him, his eyes flicking back and forth from me to the door to the window. Constant movement and awareness.

He sat on the couch across from me, his back to the bar, always looking to the windows. "Thirty-five feet is very small in high winds and big water," he said. "No friends is what I know. So, the sadness escapes me. Do you have many friends?"

"Yes," I said. "A few very close."

"And is it comforting?"

"It's helpful," I said. "Other perspectives are helpful."

"I've heard your perspectives tonight. Does that mean we are friends?" he bantered.

"Depends on whether I end up killing you, I think."

He smiled and took a drink. "Well, maybe if we don't kill each other, you can sail with me and you can take me fishing."

"Perhaps," I said.

"The transmitter signal started up again one hour after you killed Nikoli," he said, never missing a beat.

"Maybe there was a short in its electronics," I said. "That happens sometimes."

He shook his head. "I doubt it."

"Well, now you can go get your money and be gone," I said. "It was nice meeting you."

He laughed a little bit. "No, we have a meeting tomorrow morning. Nikoli's father wants to meet you," he said. He looked at his watch. He should be in the air now and will be arriving later tonight."

"He wants to meet me personally?" I asked.

"Yes. Very personal."

"I'm flattered," I said.

"You shouldn't be," he said. "So, what I thought we'd do is meet them at the transmitter location and we can retrieve the money and see what happens next."

"And where is the signal?"

He looked up at me with surprise. "Why, it's on the farm of your old friend W.B. Langford," he said. "Great place to hide treasure, on the property of a dead man."

"So what do we do until then," I asked. "Play gin rummy?"

"No, I'm leaving now. Gonna get some sleep. Been a long day." And he rose from the couch and started toward the door. "I'll see you there, say ten a.m.?"

"Sure," I said. "Wouldn't miss it for the world."

He turned and looked at me. "You are a cool one," he said. "You haven't even asked?"

"Well, we never finished the conversation about me having a gun and you having a gun and why we just don't end this thing tonight, winner take all?"

"Finally," he said. "We get to it. Because all is much too much for you, my new friend. All is a daughter in Rhode Island, a doctor, no less, who teaches at Brown University. And another daughter in Nashville who is down on her luck and easily assessable. I could give you their addresses, if you want. I can even give you their vehicle tag numbers. And those nice people in the house up the hill. No, Ethan Stewart, you won't risk all to scratch your itch for a fight. I'd bet my life on it."

"Answer me one question," I said.

"Sure."

"In the end, when you look back on your life, how do you deal with your sickening view of what is good."

"In the end, goodness always wins," he said. "For Nikoli's father, what's good is that you die." And he softly shut the door behind him and I heard Berit barking at him as he drove away.

I thought about throwing up after he left and the house was quiet again, but I poured another drink instead. There was absolutely nothing I could do. Any plan I could devise would put people I loved at great risk. John would fight and I trusted him, but he was eighteen years old. Very brave, but still eighteen. There was no way to get a crew of game wardens together by tomorrow morning that could ensure the safety of my daughters. And in the end, the Russian father wanted vengeance for his son. Justice be done. And I thought of George Acree and his lesson on vengeance and faith. I would do this alone.

I called Taylor.

"Hey," I said.

"Hey, you," she said. "You didn't see me when you were here."

"I know. The F.B.I. guy kind of ruined everything."

"You want me to come down there?" she asked.

"No. I'm really going to try and sleep. I have one more meeting tomorrow morning and then we'll celebrate."

"You sure you don't want me to come down?"

"Yeah."

"But you are okay?" she asked.

"I am."

"Well, see you tomorrow," she said.

"I love you, Taylor."

There was a long pause. "Wasn't expecting that," she said.

"Yeah, well, you already knew it. Thought I'd make it legal."

"I did know it, but it's real nice to hear," she said.

"Good," I said.

"I love you, too, Ethan."

"I know."

CHAPTER 34

I watched the sun come up through my kitchen window. The leaves were motionless on the limbs in my yard. Clear and still. I moved to the front porch and watched Berit run wide circles in the yard, chasing would-be squirrels. She came onto the porch panting and I thought about her loyalty. I sure did love that dog.

At ten a.m. I drove down the long driveway to W.B.'s house. It looked forlorn in his absence. The Crown Vic was parked beside the house and Smithson was sitting on the hood. He wore jeans and a tactical vest over a long-sleeved shirt. I parked, got out and walked up to him.

"Okay. I'm here. What's next?" I said.

"You still wearing the .45?" he asked.

"Are you?"

"Sure," he said. "But it would be best if you left yours here."

"Ain't gonna happen?" I said. "If you got a problem with that, let's just shoot each other now and be done with it. You aren't getting my gun."

"I figured," he said. "Okay, keep it. Won't do you any good, anyway. There are other eyes on you as we speak. Don't forget it."

"So, where's the alleged money?" I said.

"You really don't know?"

"When are you gonna get it through your thick skull that I don't know anything about the money. I am getting sick and tired of saying that," I said.

He pointed. "Down there. At the six hundred yard berm," he said. "Here's how we play it. We go down there and find the money. Then I call the Russians. They are close."

"Let's go," I said.

"You are an interesting man, Mr. Stewart," he said. "You are entirely too confident. You have no one here. I've had my people look. You are all alone."

"I'm used to it," I said. "Game wardens are mostly alone all the time."

We took his car and drove the farm road to the six hundred yard target. We got out and looked around. Nothing. And then we saw it, duck-taped to the back of the steel gong was the suit case. In plain sight.

He pulled a knife from his pocket and cut the tape, then threw the case on the hood of the car. "Open it," he said.

"Open it yourself," I said.

"I said open it," he said more forcefully. "Now."

I moved to the case and hit the release. It was not locked and the locks released. I opened the case and when he saw there was no bomb, he moved closer to look inside.

"Well, isn't that nice," he said.

A small transmitter lay inside. Nothing else.

"Close the case," he said.

I did.

He made a call on his cell phone and thirty seconds later another black SUV came rolling toward our position. I leaned against the car and watched as two men emerged from the vehicle and one went to the back and let an older man out. They looked so out of place on Tennessee soil. It struck me insane for them to be here. The older man looked cold, his black pants too shiny. His coat too citified. His shoes too polished. His face was hardened with wrinkles and his eyes watering. The other two men were zombies, watching his moves, and nervous, like the woods around them were the enemy. They stood close to Smithson and circled me.

The old man spoke first to Smithson. "You find money?"

"There on the hood," he said.

"This hick baboon who killed Nikoli?"

"This is Ethan Stewart, the game warden," Smithson said.

The old man walked up to me and looked me in the eyes. Hatred. He swung his right hand to slap me, but I caught his wrist easily, holding his arm. The two Russians now had their pistols out, pointing at me. The old man jerked away from me and ran to Smithson.

He yelled. "I pay you to kill him in front of me. I am here. Kill him now."

Smithson put his hand on his gun and drew it, keeping it at his side.

"Well," he said. "Kill him!"

"I don't think so," he said to the old man.

The old man looked like he had been slapped. "I have contract. You get paid. You kill him now, I say."

"He's an American," Smithson said. "I don't kill Americans."

The old man whispered something Russian to his men. One pointed his pistol at Smithson. The other turned to me and raised his weapon. And Smithson smiled, just before my man's head exploded. We heard the report of the rifle a second later. The second body guard fired at Smithson and retreated to the SUV, but didn't know which side to hide on and he chose the wrong side. The next rifle bullet took him in the neck and he collapsed at a front tire and convulsed as we heard the report of the rifle. The old man stood watching and then pulled his own gun and turned to me when Smithson shot him in the shoulder from two yards away. He secured the gun and handcuffed the old man. From behind the Crown Vic I holstered my weapon and approached Smithson. He holstered his pistol and looked up at me.

"Happened quick, huh," he said. "I never lied to you, Stewart. Just never told you all the truth," he said.

I hit him with all my weight and it knocked him backwards and he rolled to a stop. He lay there for a second, before shaking his head, as if to clear it. He finally sat up and then waved me off. "Wait a second. Just wait a second," he said. Pulling a phone from his pocket, he dialed a number.

"All clear," he said. "Come on down."

He looked up at me and his eye was already swelling badly. "You would have never trusted my snipers," he said. "You would have never agreed to do it."

'I ought to break your neck," I said. "Who are you?"

He stood and faced me. "Don't hit me again or I'll shoot you, Stewart."

"Answer my question," I said.

"Do you think you are the only law enforcement with a stake in this thing? You are a pompous ass, Stewart. Two guys have died working undercover with this operation. Two years we have been working it and only when you killed Tiller Mabry did we have an opening that would work?"

"What are you talking about?" I said.

"Vengeance," he said. "Vengeance caught that old man. I have him now on tape telling me to kill you. Admitting he paid money to have you killed. We had two hours of him on tape hiring me, but he never said the words. "You have a Federal commission, right?"

"Yes," I said.

"So now we have him contracting to kill a federal officer. That's even better."

"So you are with the F.B.I?"

"No," he said. "But I am with the federal government and that is all you're gonna find out. So sit your ass down and wait 'till my guys come off that hill way over there and thank them for being the finest snipers this side of Afghanistan which saved your ass."

"What about the money?" I asked.

"We don't care about the money," he said. "Hell, Tiller probably spent it all anyway. We used the money to get Nikoli down here to save his honor with his father."

I looked at the old man on the ground. "You better give him some help. He'll go into shock and die on you."

Smithson walked over to the old man, who was mumbling Russian with his eyes closed. "I just grazed him," he said. "He'll live."

I looked in the distance and saw three men approaching off the hill. Two in front and one in the rear.

"I thought you said two snipers," I said.

He looked and saw the three men. "What the hell," he said, running to his vehicle and getting a pair of binoculars.

"Who is that guy? The one in the rear?"

"Let me see," I said. And he handed me the glasses.

I smiled. "Calm down," I said. "He's friendly."

"Who is he?"

"That's John Russell," I said. "The kid you met last night at Taylor's house."

"What the hell is he doing here?" he said.

"I don't know, and that's the truth."

"Let me see those glasses," he said taking them from me. He looked again. "My guys are tied and gagged," he said. "The kid has a shotgun."

"That would be John," I said smiling.

As they neared, John sat the two camo-clad officers on the ground and approached by himself.

"I found them like that," he said. "Wasn't sure whether you wanted me to untie them or not," he said. "So I just marched 'em down here when they got the call."

"Was that you that answered the phone?" Smithson asked.

"Well, it was ringing," John said.

"That's fine, John," I said. "If they were tied, who did the shooting?" I said.

"Couldn't truthfully say," he said. "Wasn't me."

"Just what in the hell are you doing here," Smithson said.

John looked strangely at the man, like he was confused at the question. "Squirrel hunting, sir. I love squirrels and dumplins. So, who's the dead guys?" he asked looking at the men on the ground.

"Bull shit," Smithson said.

Smithson yelled at the men to come down and they stood up shakily and approached us. Smithson pulled the gags from their mouths and cut the duck tape around their wrists. They were both big men and looked more like soldiers than lawmen.

"Speak," Smithson said.

The older man rubbed his wrists. "We've been tied since sunup," he said. "Snuck up on us without a sound, knocked us both unconscious and stole the bolts from our rifles. Sorry, sir, but we never saw it coming."

"Whoever hit you did the shooting?"

"Yes sir. About a hundred yards from our position. Behind us. I figure seven hundred yards."

"You listen to me, men, and I mean listen," Smithson said.

"Yes sir."

"You did the shooting. You understand me. You did the shooting just like we planned."

"Yes sir."

"You got a problem with that?" he said to me.

"Nope," I said.

"You, boy?"

"No, sir," John said.

Smithson looked at me. "You damn game wardens are dangerous," he said. "I've got a ghost shooter who thankfully was on our side. I don't know who he is and don't really care. The plan worked."

And he reached into his vehicle, coming out with a radio and called for backup. In three minutes, we heard the helicopter coming over the trees at the far end of the valley.

"**I**'m going home," I said to Smithson. "You know where to find me."

Smithson tried to smile, but it didn't look like one with his eye swollen shut. "Fine," he said. "I'll be in touch. And Stewart, I'm sorry about the con, but admit it. You wouldn't have done it, if we had asked."

"Absolutely not," I said. "But admit this; your little plan almost got you killed."

Smithson paused, wheels turning.

"Think about it," I said. "Whoever the shooter was didn't know you were on my side or your guys wouldn't have been bushwhacked. Think about your head if you had pointed the gun at me," I said.

"But I didn't," he said. "And by the way, it was a good plan. We got it from you. Just letting them do what they do and we were protecting ourselves."

"Your protection was duck-taped and gagged," I said. "Great plan, Smithson. Brilliant." I turned to John. "C'mon John, I'll give you a ride." And we walked away toward W.B.'s old house. After a hundred yards I whispered. "Nice shooting."

"Wasn't me," he said.

"Okay. If that's how you want to play it. I'm still impressed."

"I'm telling you. Wasn't me."

"Look," I said. "W.B. told me he taught you to shoot long range. He said you were real good."

"He did," he said. "And I am, but I didn't do it."

"Well, y'all are the only ones I know who could make those shots, and he's dead. So who else could it be?"

"You wouldn't believe me if I told you," he said.

CHAPTER 35

There were no news stories covering the shootings. Amazing how the Feds can keep things quiet, but they do. It was as if the events of the morning never happened. We were given gag orders by the F.B I. and sworn to secrecy, under penalty of some federal code, regarding on-going investigations. John and I were fine with that. I was told my testimony would be needed in Federal Court, but it might be a year before it came to trial. They wanted nothing in testimony from John, as his presence on the scene only led to the ghost shooter, which they wanted to forget entirely.

So, the four of us sat on the back porch of the big house in the late afternoon drinking wine and for the first time in a long time, relaxing. All the dogs were loose in the yard, fighting and running, and playing. Seems they were happy too.

John and Julia were sitting on the steps and he was playing his guitar. Julia was trying to sing a Garth Brooks song...poorly, but John didn't care and she was happy with her voice, like singing in the shower.

Taylor moved behind me and rubbed my shoulders and her hands were strong and purposeful. "I love this place," she said.

I took her hands and centered them on my chest. "This place is worthy of love," I said. "We are very lucky to be here right now in this place with each other."

"What do you think they will do now?" she asked.

"I hope they both go to college and get married and have some kids that can be lucky too," I said. "In that order."

She moved to the table and sipped her wine, looking at me the whole time. "What about us?"

"Well, if you'll accompany me, we're going on a short vacation."

"Really?" she said smiling. "Where to?"

"The mountains of northern New Mexico," I said. "So, are you up for a road trip?"

"With you by my side?" she said.

"With me never leaving your side," I said.

"Then I'm all in," she said.

I lifted my glass and she touched it with hers.

"You ever been there?" I said.

"Nope. Not New Mexico."

"I was born there, you know," I said.

"No," she said. "You never told me."

"Yeah, some border town called Hobbs. My father started out in the pipeline valve business and that's where they lived when I was born. Opposite direction than we're going."

"Did you like it?"

"I have no memories of it," I said. "We moved around. Became a Tennessean when I was eleven, when they came home and stayed."

"I didn't know," she said. "There's lots we don't know, huh?"

"We have time," I said. And she smiled at me. "But," I continued, "I have hiked these northern mountains in my adult life and I must warn you, the mountains in summer are very romantic. They might sweep you off your feet."

"I doubt it," she said. "Already been swept."

CHAPTER 36

Three days later, we caught a Southwest flight out of Nashville to Albuquerque, rented a Ford Explorer, and were headed north to Sante Fe. I had told Taylor to pack lightly, which led to numerous questions about our activities to ensure the right clothes would be packed. I told her I had no idea what we would do. I also suggested neither heels nor pearls were needed. Jeans and comfortable shoes would do nicely.

I had a medium size bag. She had two large bags to cover all the possibilities. I had just smiled and given up. But she did look wonderful sitting in the right seat, studying a country so different than the hills and hollows of Tennessee, with its New Mexico tans and browns and cedar-like greens dotting the landscape. I learned she could not sit still, and changed positions often, sometimes sitting cross-legged facing me as we talked. And talked. And talked...

From Sante Fe we headed north toward the Colorado border passing through towns named Abiquiu and Tierra Amarilla. My GPS led the way to the coordinates I entered, the same numbers scribbled in the bottom of W.B.'s box. We were close.

After several miles on a lonely road we came to an unlocked gate and a ranch road that led across a remote valley. I chanced the trespassing charge and took the road, following the GPS.

"Do you know where we are?" she said.

"No."

"Do you know what we will find?"

"No."

"Then why are we here?"

"A hunch," I said.

We topped a small rise and in the distance, I saw it. I stopped. We took in the view. A neat little red caboose with a wooden rail fence in front and a small red tack barn to the side, butted under the rise of the mountain behind. No sign of anyone.

I drove forward a half mile and parked in front of the caboose. We got out and stretched. The view was wonderful and we scanned the land around us for any sign of life. But there was none. Pasture and wildflowers of purple and red between huge rocks and tree lines of mature aspen and conifers lay under a huge sky of deep blue over us.

"This is beautiful," she said.

"It is," I said.

"So, you think I might find out what we are doing here anytime soon?"

"We might have to wait a while," I said.

"For what?"

"The caboose is definitely lived in," I said. "It's too neat."

"Yeah," she said. "For a man."

"That's because it's not a man," I said. "Her name is Louise. I need to talk to her about W.B."

"She knew him?"

"W.B. carved her name in a rock back home. I suspect so."

"W.B. Langford carved a woman's name in a rock?"

"Saw it with my own eyes," I said.

"Amazing," she said. "So we wait?"

"You okay with it?"

"Long as it doesn't last over a week or two," she said. "Berit will think we've abandoned her."

An hour later, we were sitting on the hood of the Explorer, our backs leaning against the windshield. We had been studying the clouds, something I had not done since childhood. In the distance we saw two horses with riders and one dog walking slowly off the distant hill.

"That wasn't too long," she said.

"If that's her," I said.

She paused. "Do you have your gun?"

I turned to her and looked disappointed.

"Stupid question," she said.

And we watched for another twenty minutes as the riders came closer, never changing their course, or speed, constantly getting larger in our vision until a hundred yards away. I slid off the hood and Taylor stood beside me, waiting.

"Well, John was right," I whispered.

"What?"

"I don't believe it."

I heard the horses, their feet in the grass, the creaking leather of the saddles, the dog barking now, as they closed to ten yards and stopped.

"Magger," the woman on the horse said to the Border Collie. The dog circled the horse and sat beside her. She sat the horse comfortably, watching me. She wore a single-action Colt pistol in a well worn holster, and for the life of me, I could not tell where the woman was separated from the horse and the horse from the ground and the dog. They were all one thing, bonded by some wonderful harmony of mountain movement, like the swaying of an aspen in the breeze.

"Ma'am," I said. And I turned my eyes to the man next to her. "You get off that horse and I'm gonna knock your damn fool head off."

The woman on the horse moved her hand to her pistol, her thumb on the hammer.

Taylor said to me, but they could hear. "May be just womanly intuition, but that woman will shoot you."

W.B. smiled. "Well, that's true, Miss James. It's also true that I'm not quite as dead as I let on." He paused. "Louise, meet Ethan Stewart and Miss Taylor James. They are friends I told you about. And if he hits me, don't shoot him. Reckon I deserve it."

Louise half-smiled and moved her hand away from the gun. "Pleased," she said and touched her hat.

W.B. began to dismount and I walked toward him. When his feet hit the ground and he turned, I hit him as hard as I could with a right cross. It connected and he fell against the horse, which shied and then the dog was barking again. W.B. never went down. He worked his jaw to make sure it wasn't broken, and then smiled at me it out his hand.

"Now, are we okay?" he said.

I shook my head. "You got some explaining to do," I said.

"And best done over brown whiskey and mule deer backstrap. I guarantee you the best you ever laid a lip to," he said. "But for the record, I never claimed to be dead. Just said I wasn't coming home. And if you'll think about it, that's all Doc said. W.B. ain't coming home from Houston."

"We had your damn funeral," I said.

"I know," he said. "I was there. Now that's something every man should get to do. Attend his own funeral. Eye-opening experience," he said.

"You were there?"

"Hell, Ethan, of course I was. You think I'd of missed it. Stayed in the shadows. Nobody noticed."

"People hurt because of your death, W.B."

"I know," he said. "And that hurt me, but you have to understand, I had no idea anybody'd even come to my funeral, much less grieve."

"Then you're not half as smart as I gave you credit," I said.

"Dumber'n box of turtles," he said. "I was that."

"And your cancer? Was that fake, too.?"

"Nope," he said. "Them boys in Houston found out I didn't have cancer. Histoplasmosis, they said. Symptoms sometimes mimic the cancer. Got it cured with antibiotics. I'm fit as a fiddle."

"What about the shooting on your place?" I said.

W.B. raises his hands. "Whoa, Chief. What's your rush? Look, y'all get in that vehicle and follow that little road across that creek and up the side of that hill. After about a mile, you'll come to the elk camp. Meet us up there. We'll get supplies and drink and eat 'till sunup if you want. Fair enough?"

I smiled and grabbed him like a lost brother and the two women watched us and began laughing. W.B. took the reins of his horse and started toward the barn.

"W.B.," Taylor said.

He stopped, turned to her and was still smiling.

"If I may say, I haven't known you long, but I never even saw you smile before," Taylor said. "You look happy. That's real nice."

"Ma'am," he said. "I'm so happy my teeth are sunburned."

At the elk camp, sitting around a large fire pit in comfortable chairs, we had drinks and watched the mule deer steaks sizzle on the grill. The wood cracked as it burned and we sat up-wind of the smoke. The sun was gone and the stars were brilliant overhead. I never asked another question, figuring W.B. would talk when ready. And finally, he sighed and said, "Okay, Ethan. Fire away. I'll go through this once and then it's past, never to be spoke of again. Deal?"

"Deal," I said. "Were you the shooter at your place?"

He tossed a twig in the fire and followed it with his eyes. "Of course I was. I felt pretty safe, being dead and all."

"Yeah, but how could you possibly know to come back?"

"I had one person who knew I was alive. It had to go that way. I couldn't leave without being sure I could get back if you needed me."

"So, you thought it might not be over?"

"My gut told me, no," he said.

"And the one person. That would be John," I said.

"John," he said. "But he didn't know until after the funeral. I contacted him and explained enough to settle him down and then gave a contact number. He called me after your meeting at the boat ramp. When you told him to put his gun back on. I came then."

"How? If you're dead, what do you use for I.D. to fly?"

W.B. laughed. "Hell, Chief, you're thinking too hard. I ain't dead. I still got my I.D. Airlines don't know anything about this."

"What about money? You left it all to John."

"I got plenty of money," he said. "But let's get back to the shooting. That was tricky, 'cause all I knew was you killed the Russians. I figured the only way to bait the trap was to reactivate the transmitter, and see what happened. Of course I put it where I was comfortable, which was my old place."

"So, you stole Tiller's money?" I said.

"Of course I did," he said. "I had to compensate Samuel's family for what he did to them. Amanda and those kids are set up real nice for a long time. And I mean real nice."

I shook my head. "How'd you find it?"

"The money?"

"Yeah."

"I had been shadowing Tiller before you even came to Houston County," he said. "You remember, I had my own plan to kill him."

"He never knew you were on him?"

W.B. looked at me like he was hurt. "Of course not," he said. "That boy was so caught up with himself he thought he was bulletproof. Buried the money in an old cabin at Leatherwood."

I sipped my whiskey and thought some more. "How'd you know to set up on the very day we showed up?"

"I was prepared to wait as long as it took after turning the transmitter back on, but John called after the F.B.I came to your house. Said something was wrong, cause you told him to make sure and feed the dogs. He said it hurt his feelings at first, but then knew it was a warning, cause you knew he would never let his dogs go hungry."

"I was spooked when the F.B.I. just showed up," I said. "He could have called. There was no reason for him just to show up, especially by himself. But what about the shooters? How'd you know they weren't bad guys?"

"You mean besides the fact they spoke American and wore American camo?" he said. "That was pretty easy. They had cops written all over them."

"Why didn't you just let them do the shooting?"

"Hell, I didn't know how good they were, and wasn't absolutely sure they weren't dirty. Thought I'd play it safe and bonk 'em good. Do the shooting myself."

He turned the steaks on the grill with a big fork and sat back down. "Anything else?"

"How come you didn't shoot the F.B.I. guy? I didn't know he was a good guy 'till the shooting started."

W.B. smiled. "That was easier. After the Russians were shot and he was still standing, I figured you didn't want him dead or you would have killed him."

We listened to the fire for a minute. I turned to Louise, who sat stoically beside W.B. patting her dog. "You know he carved your name on a rock in Tennessee," I said.

She looked quickly at him and then back at me. "Okay," she said.

"Well, what do you think about this big tough guy doing something romantic like that?"

"What I think about that would be none of your business," she said.

Taylor laughed out loud and toasted her drink toward Louise. "Way to go, Louise," she said.

I toasted them both. "Y'all will do well together," I said.

After the laughter left us and the fire talked some more I said, "One more question?"

He just looked at me.

"You're not smoking?" I said. "You quit?"

"Yep," he said quickly. "The Lord told me to."

I blinked. "Really?"

"Yep. After Houston and my sudden recovery, I started reading the Bible. Didn't know what I was looking for, but I kept reading. This Jesus feller, well you hear he's a personal savior. Heard that my whole life, but it never took. When I read the part about Him throwing them sons of bitches out of the temple backing his daddy's play, well He spoke to me, then. And I quit."

I smiled.

"Well, W.B.," Taylor said. "That's the first time in my whole life I've ever heard the story told quite like that."

W.B. shrugged. "The truth is the truth," he said.

"What did Jesus say about shooting people?" I asked.

He smiled. "We ain't spoke of it yet. But I'll listen, if He does."

Later that night, after supper and drinks, W.B. and Louise rode back to the caboose with the dog. Taylor and I sat up a long time around the fire, before retiring to a pile of blankets they had brought us, staring up at the stars and counting the ones that shot across the sky.

"Hey."

"Hey, you," she said.

"You ever seen stars look so close?"

"Never," she said.

"You happy?"

"If the sun was out, my teeth would be sunburned," she giggled.

"Me, too," I said. "Me, too.

CHAPTER 37

I woke up the next morning wrapped in the blankets with Taylor, smelling bacon and coffee. When I rolled over and looked behind me, W.B. was sitting at the fire cooking.

"Y'all gonna sleep all day?" he said.

I tried to get up but was all bent. Taylor pulled the blanket over her head and disappeared. I stood, but not straight and walked stiffly to the fire.

"Thought I'd be hospitable and fix your breakfast. Didn't figure you brought food."

"No," I said getting a cup of coffee. "We didn't."

"Well, the railroad car is quite small, so can't offer you a place to sleep, lessen you want to stay up here. That'd be fine."

He poured a half a dozen eggs in the bacon grease and commenced to stirring. "Check that Dutch oven and see if the biscuits are brown."

I scraped the coals off the lid and raised it to see perfectly browned biscuits, so I pulled the oven from the fire and set it on the table.

"I guess we'll head back to Sante Fe and find a nice place there for a few days," I said.

"No need," he said. "Louise found a place for you. She has a friend that owns a spread over the mountain. Ain't far but will take you several hours to get there by the roads. Rich family out of Denver owns it. She looks after it while they're gone. She made a call last night and made arrangements. I think it'll work." He reached in his shirt pocket and produced a set of keys. "Big key gets through the gate on the road. Little one the house." He handed them to me with a crude hand-sketched map. "Leave them buried by the north side of the mailbox post when you leave. We'll pick 'em up."

"That's very nice of her," I said. "Where is she?"

"She left before sun-up heading that way," he said pointing behind him. "Checking cattle. She said to tell you to come back sometime and stay awhile."

"We will W.B.," I said. "We will."

He scraped the eggs in two plates beside the bacon and placed them on the table next to the forks. "We'll stop by later and clean up, but if you'd tend the fire before you leave, I'd appreciate it."

"You leaving?"

"Yeah. Try to catch up with her. Miss her already," he said smiling. "And that's a new thing for me. Kinda like it."

"I understand," I said. "Your jaw okay?"

He rubbed it. "Yeah, but you hit pretty good for a desk- riding Chief."

"You take care of yourself, W.B. I'm gonna miss you."

"Of course you will," he said. "But you got John. He's a pretty good second. Do your best to guide him straight, Ethan. I promised his momma."

"I will do that," I said.

"And two more things that didn't get said last night," he said. "First, I told you when I died I'd leave you that .308 rifle. So, in the future, if you don't have the gun, I ain't dead. And second, how much money they say Tiller took?"

"Seven hundred and fifty thousand," I said.

He threw his head back and laughed.

"That's not right?" I said.

"Yeah," he said. "Seven hundred and fifty thousand in each case. There were two."

We followed the map W.B. gave me and arrived mid-afternoon. I unlocked the gate, pulled through and locked it behind me. We traveled a ranch road for two miles through two creeks and several large stands of aspen, and finally the valley opened before us. There was a large lake, maybe two hundred acres, tucked against the mountain and one house overlooking it. A large glass-fronted structure with a huge front porch was not what I expected. It had a huge rock fireplace on one side. A flock of teal got up off the lake as we approached with their fast moving little wings glittering against the water.

"That's no hunting shack," I said.

"We're staying there?" she said.

"I think so," I said. "I hope so."

We climbed the steps to the deck and I tried the key to the front door. It worked. We entered. We stared.

The room was enormous. Hard wood floors and massive timbers supported the structure. The rock fireplace was thirty feet in height. The room itself was uncluttered and decorated with American Indian art on the walls. A full kitchen and bar was positioned against the far wall and steps going up to a second story. We climbed the steps and explored the upstairs. A spacious master bedroom looked at the lake below with its own deck and chairs. We opened the glass door to the deck and stepped outside. Leaning against the wooden railing, the breeze off the mountain touched us and moved her hair.

"Think it's for sale?" she said.

"I wouldn't sell it if it were mine," I said.

"You have a point," she said. "Think the shower works?" she said.

"I'll get the bags. You find out."

By dusk, we had showered, changed clothes and found food and drink in great abundance in the kitchen. By dark we were on the bedroom deck, feet propped on the rail, saying nothing, sipping our drinks.

"I thought we lived in the country," she whispered.

"Explain," I said.

"No lights here, except the stars. No sounds, except the wind. Almost divine silence. No cars, trucks, trains, or boats. Just this beauty," she said.

"And us."

"And us," she said.

"Did you sleep any last night?" I asked.

"I was happy to not sleep with you under those blankets and watch the stars," she said.

"Me either," I said. "You tired?"

"Not so much," she said. And she stood. "I'll be back."

I stood there for a long time, it seemed, pondering the effects of water on the soul. The moon soon crested the nearest mountain and cast its shimmering light across the lake. I pondered God and how patient He must be in our wanderings for the truth. I pondered W.B. and his fate with life and death. I thought about how lucky I had been in the people who had crossed my path while I searched for answers, particularly those who chose to walk by my side. The moonlight was brilliant across the water and wanting Taylor to see, I turned back to the room, which now had one candle burning by the bed.

"Taylor," I said. "Come here."

When I saw her, she was wearing something sheer and in the filtering moonlight, her naked silhouette very visible. She said nothing but walked my way, each step bringing the vision nearer, until up close I could smell her freshness, like new flowers.

"I'm here," she whispered.

"I'll say," I whispered back.

And she moved in front of me looking toward the night and I wrapped my arms around her, feeling the softness of her, breathing through her hair, watching the moonlight on the water.

"It's something to behold," I whispered. "There is something about watching the water. I haven't quite figured it out yet, but it soothes me."

"I turned the bed back," she said. "We can see the water from inside."

"I won't be watching the water from inside," I said.

"I think not," she whispered. "But later, it will be soothing."

She held my hands in hers and we stood there a long time.

"I want you to know that I wasn't looking for you when I found you," I said.

She kissed my hand. "That's funny," she whispered.

"What?"

"I've been looking for you since I was fourteen," she whispered.

"I'm not going anywhere," I said.

She turned and kissed me softly. "Yes, you are," she said. And she took my hand and led me through the door and I followed her, my heart pounding....

ACKNOWLEDGMENTS

Any work of fiction involves a series of imaginary events which sometimes work wonderfully when placed on the page and merge with characters in a believable way to pull the reader deeper into the story. These events and dialogues are many times in need of a truthful review by those whose opinions are valued by the writer and may promote changes or modifications which add valuably to the story. For all my trusted friends who I have asked opinions about my words, I thank you. And particularly, I want to thank Jerry Strom for his friendship during the early story development. Also, my thanks to Jay Langston for his help over the years in getting these written words actually into the hands of readers.

ABOUT THE AUTHOR

Gary Cook is a nationally recognized, award-winning short-story author who worked for thirty-four years as a wildlife professional in Tennessee. His first novel, *Wounded Moon*, set in the mountains of East Tennessee, received critical acclaim. *Chance of Rain* is his second novel.

Gary lives with his wife, Karen, in western Tennessee.

Made in the USA
Middletown, DE
01 September 2020